LUCANUS

PRODIGAL SON

BOOK 3 OF THE UNWINDING

JULIANA REW

Cover Art by Keely Rew

Lucanus: Prodigal Son
The Unwinding Series Book 3

by Juliana Rew

Copyright 2021 Sophont Press
ISBN #978-1-7362848-4-1

Discover other titles by Juliana Rew:

The Unwinding Series
The Unwinding: Gin's Story
Extremophile: Violet Rain

Dragon Stead Series
Erenarch Academy: Under the Dragon Banner
Daris Moon
Miranda of Daris

Mountain Ma'am
The Adventures of Mountain Ma'am

License Notes

Cover: Keely Rew

www.julianarew.com

Dedication

For everyone who hopes those twinkly lights in the night sky aren't all that far away.

Contents

*****~~~~~*****

PART I. EXPIATION

The Empire is in its third century. Living is not a worry, because all needs are taken care of by the One God, Masquat. It has been eight years since your child was called to leave on the Divine Campaign. You had no choice but to let him go—children are no longer the property of their parents, after all. But in your subconscious, the guilt plays over and over.

Chapter 1.

The Children's Crusade

Lu Qiang ignored the itch on the back of his neck from the wool uniform issued to new trainees and tried to keep from joyfully skipping to the chief warrant officer's desk to report for duty. He'd been chosen for his maturity, after all. Even though he was only eight years old, he'd argued persuasively with his mother to be given permission to join the space corps and go on the next interstellar children's crusade. He would be one of the youngest, well below the age of consent, which was thirteen. Plus, with his genetic improvements, he was well qualified to work in both zero and high gravity.

"Name?"

"Lu Qiang. Sir."

The chief warrant officer glanced up. Lu Qiang straightened to attention. He hoped it was an approving glance.

"Miss your Mother, do you, boy?"

"What? No, sir. I'm reporting for duty."

"I certainly miss mine. Just a joke, son, probably the last one you'll hear from me. Ah, here you are. Sign on this line. You can write, can't you?"

Lu Qiang started to object that—*of course, he could write his own name!* But then he realized that it was another joke. The man obviously was making fun of him. He nodded curtly and scribbled his name on the crew manifest. He handed it back to the officer, who promptly dropped it.

"Sorry, I'm a bit wobbly today," the warrant officer said, snatching it off the floor. "I've been on one too many missions, probably."

Too many missions. The officer wasn't old, he looked twenty at most. Was that a warning? Lu Qiang wondered how old the man really was. Time on interstellar voyages at near-relativistic speeds didn't appear to pass as quickly as on Sheba-4, but the mind was said to have its own internal clock.

"Here is your netlink. You'll get all your orders and communications with it. Learn how to use it, and don't ever lose it," the officer said. Lu Qiang had actually used a much newer model at home. "You're Group G. Report to B Deck…Next."

Lu Qiang had no idea how to get to B deck, but before he could ask, another boy took his place at the front of the line, so he was on his own to figure it out.

B Deck housed the crew, and was one level down. He wondered how many levels there were. The ships in the vids looked like they had at least a dozen. Eventually he found a room labeled G. He would share the room with five other boys, each assigned a different six-hour shift during the thirty-hour ship days. Another boy lounged nearby, playing a game on the tiny screen of his netlink.

"Hello, I'm Lu Qiang," he said.

"Periot. You can stow your gear in a foot locker under a bunk. Don't leave your stinky wet socks lying around, or you'll get docked." Lu Qiang dropped his bag, but had no time to become settled, when he was summoned to duty. His netlink buzzed.

ALL CREW SCRAMBLE. THIS IS NOT A DRILL.

His shift hadn't begun yet, but this was a call for all hands. Periot rubbed his eyes and clambered out of his bunk, slipping his feet into his boots.

"What's going on?" Lu Qiang asked Periot, who had been the last one on shift.

"Maybe the test didn't go so well," Periot responded. "Dammit, I was hoping to get some rest."

"What test?"

"It's a new way to travel down a wormhole. The problem is, they don't know how to get back, so there's no way to see if it succeeds, except to send someone to the other end and see if they can return. I'm just glad I wasn't chosen for the test."

Lu Qiang nodded, pushing down on the handle to open the heavy door. It took all his strength. "I remember the Emperor saying we're close to moving to a higher plane," he said to himself."

They queued up in the hall and waited for a turn to climb the ladders to Deck A for assembly. When they arrived, about a hundred child soldiers were gathering into their groups.

"Where's Rankle?" Periot said. "He's supposed to be on shift now."

The warrant officer moved to the front. Lu Qiang had nicknamed him "Wobbly" behind his back, and couldn't suppress a smile.

"What are you gobs grinning at?" Wobbly said. "Group G, move forward."

Lu Qiang gulped. How had Group G gotten so close to the front? Apparently Wobbly knew about alliteration too. Lu Qiang snapped to attention.

"We have made progress on the wormhole testing," the warrant officer reported. "We have established communication with the test ship, which broadcast a location beacon. The signal frequency slowed as the ship went into the singularity, as expected. However, we have been unable to talk to the crew. For all practical purposes, the wormhole is one-way. We need volunteers to bring them back."

Lu Qiang's mouth fell open. From the sound of it, the test crew might have perished. What, were they asking for people to go down a one-way path to their deaths?

Periot leaned over to whisper in his ear. "Whatever you do, don't volunteer for anything."

"Our goal is to dramatically shorten travel time around the nearby solar systems, and this test demonstrated that we definitely can," the warrant officer continued. "We believe the testers are now located at their destination. By design, we calculate that we can reach them by rocket in thirty-nine days, or around eighty days for the whole trip."

Periot said under his breath, "I don't see how eighty days by rocket is a dramatic reduction." Periot was the oldest in the group, and he was good with numbers.

Lu Qiang raised his hand. "Is this the higher plane the Emperor was talking about?"

"Indeed it is, my lad. Thank you for volunteering."

"Dammit, I told you…" Periot said.

Lu Qiang was beginning to wish he'd never come. He wished his mother had tried harder to dissuade him. He could be home, petting his puppy and watching the latest shows on the nightly news vids. Those vids had been his downfall, all tales about fame and glory, with no grownups to constantly pester you to come home promptly after school and spend the rest of the day studying. And now he'd "volunteered." He was going to die for sure.

☙

But Lu Qiang didn't die, although many of his shipmates did. The first nearly forty-day solo rocket trip seemed uneventful, except for the crushing gravity that would kill an unenhanced human. His ship carried extra fuel and food for the doubly long trip home at regular gravity, assuming a test crew had survived. It turned out that was unnecessary.

Lu Qiang's ship accelerated to a quarter of the speed of light for 20 days, then braked to a stop for the remaining distance. He was a little afraid that he might find a bloody mess, having heard from Periot that anything going into a black hole would be "spaghettified"—stretched impossibly thin, like a rubber band. To Lu Qiang's surprise, there was no ship. No blood. No pink slime. Just *nothing*. The test crew had simply disappeared. The Empire fleet commander hadn't bothered to give details, intent on arranging the rocket rescue. As the horror of the fate of his unknown shipmates set in, the words of the petty officer came back to him, "Miss your Mother, do you, boy?" He wished he had asked for her blessing.

Lu Qiang prepared to report back. "Listen, I know this isn't what you want to hear, but there's no one here."

He was lucky. Extraordinarily lucky. Everyone said so. He could have been placed on a test crew. The next test had similar "bloody spaghetti" results, yet Lu Qiang was always selected to be on the "rescue" mission. The longer it went on, the more unmoored from reality he felt. A cinder of dissatisfaction grew to a burning anger. His lucky escape had turned into an endless journey with only one itinerary: to Hell and back.

Not satisfied with the vague explanations offered by the Emperor's Scientist artificial intelligence robots, he demanded to learn more about the research behind the wormhole project. At first, the Scientists resisted. Math hadn't been Lu Qiang's forte as a young student, but there was little else to do on these trips except study, so he gradually gained more of what the Scientists referred to as "mathematical maturity."

Finally, after he had nearly lost count, Lu Qiang boarded the latest test pod and found the crew alive. He communicated the good news back to his transport ship. The Empire would have its wormhole shuttle system at last.

Now it should be just a matter of building another wormhole for the return trip. Lu Qiang studied the details of the latest successful test and felt hopeful for the first time. He realized that, along with the Empire, he had mastered the powerful secret they had been seeking.

Hell was no longer the default destination. However, neither was Sheba-4. The Empire had claimed a dozen planets in the nearby quadrant. Without wormhole transport, most were remote enough that the Empire's control was weak at best. Lu Qiang had only contempt for the Empire's careless objectification of its children as "scientific test subjects." The religious crusade was nothing but a sham. Without informing the Empire fleet commander, Lu Qiang built another dozen wormholes. He explained to the test crew that they now had the choice to traverse one of the newly constructed holes and make a start on a different planet. It was obvious that even if the crew returned to Sheba-4, they might be reassigned for further dangerous missions. Lu Qiang ferried those who chose to desert to their chosen destinations. He didn't go with them. Though he knew they would make it through alive, he needed time to think. To think about what the technique meant for the future of the Empire. None of those colonies appealed to him. What was it all for, anyway? He would again take the long way back to the ship, for old time's sake. In deep cold sleep, he dreamed of swaying daisies beneath a yellow sun.

After Lu Qiang returned to the ship, he asked to go home to Sheba-4, and his request was granted promptly.

They all treated him differently. They saluted and called him Lucanus. He bore the DNA imprint of the Emperor, after all. He wondered when *that* had happened.

❧

Shan-Lien finished her prayers to Masquat, asking for blessings for herself and her son. She snatched a warm red scarf from the peg and threw it over her shoulders. She had to hurry. The transport was due within the hour, carrying spoils from the returning crusade, and, if she was lucky, news of her son. She called the dog inside, and told him to be good, she'd be right back. He shook off misting rain, exuding a familiar wet-fur smell. *Lu Qiang's puppy, now middle-aged.*

A taxi nosed out of traffic and waited while she climbed in for the trip to the airfield. With time dilation, Lu Qiang would have aged slowly relative to those here on Sheba-4, and she should still be able to recognize him, assuming his ship hadn't ventured too far. When he'd left there were only half a dozen planets within a reasonable distance for missionary work.

She reminded herself that she must call her son "Lucanus," not her private nickname, "Luqas." The latter undignified but somehow more appropriate name had come to her in a dream as she waited the long months until the delivery.

But now the Empire had added another triumph to its sacred quest. *Triumph?* To Shan-Lien, it seemed more like raiding, though she'd never say so aloud. The Emperor Li Wei had assumed the name "Calaneris," to show his admiration for the rulers of an ancient empire. He insisted their child now be called Lucanus. She hoped the boy hadn't been re-upped. She might be dead before he returned from a second mission.

She didn't care about herself, of course. That would be unworthy. Her sacrifice was for the good of all. But it just seemed wrong to send children on these crusades. Of course, the distances involved were so large that if anything

13

went wrong only those who could live through the sub-light speed trip out and back were chosen.

Out. And back... Shan-Lien shivered. Most of the children Lucanus's age had gone and never returned. Innocents—martyrs, to be sure, but it felt ineffably sad nonetheless. Was the sacrifice required to convert the non-enlightened a noble goal? She was of two minds. But word was that they'd made a working wormhole, and a ship was bringing its crew home.

She hoped—no, she was sure—Lucanus would be on this one, and she'd be reunited with her son. Dressing that morning, she'd contemplated her reflection in the mirror. Liberal daily supplements of life-extending spermidine and cadaverine had helped her defray the ravages of aging, but a few wrinkles had crept to the corners of her eyes, and gray hairs streaked through the black. What would Lu Qiang—Lucanus—think of her? Old and in the way? How old would he be, relatively speaking?

Crowds gathered outside the mesh fences of the landing field of the royal city of Megali. The mesh was transparent for now, but would go dark when the ship was safe on the ground. A brief quarantine, while the authorities took a look at who—or what—was inside.

Shan-Lien felt in her pocket for the pass that would allow her inside the perimeter. Her hands were sweaty, in spite of the cold. Luckily the coating on the pass was permeable, so that her residual DNA could be sampled and read. There were some advantages to being a cousin of the Emperor.

She left the taxi and worked her way through the throng.

"Documentation, please." The guard was polite. The red scarf she wore identified her as a Mother, though in her case that was really just a polite word for concubine. Shan-Lien whisked a forefinger of gloss over her mouth, whose lips had not been used for kissing in a long time. She feared the years had not been kind to her. She looked up as a cheer rose from the crowd, shading her eyes from the brilliant light descending toward them. A whirlwind of dust blew over the group of waiting dignitaries and relatives, choking them in a fog of hydrocarbons. Even with interstellar flight, they still needed rockets to slow their plummet into the planet's gravity well.

The group started forward, but guards held them back. "Wait, make room for the cargo transports."

Shan-Lien stamped her feet, only partly to keep warm. She told herself to be patient. She'd waited this long, a few minutes more wouldn't hurt. The crowd murmured excitedly, anticipating the announcement of the Empire's greatest achievement.

She thought about her last glimpse of little Luqas, as he boarded this very same ship, the snapshot as clear in her mind as eight years ago. He was so handsome. It had been sixteen years since her cousin offered to give her a child of her—their—his—own. He would contribute DNA in return for a partage of the child, though ownership was technically forbidden under the religion they shared. She'd agreed instantly. Why did her beautiful child want to run away from his destiny?

For ordinary citizens, it would be fiendishly expensive, but the Emperor could afford it. Calaneris summoned the finest child-designer AI available from among his cadre of Scientists, programmed to apply state-of-the-art gene editing to ensure a perfect baby. Shan-Lien and Calaneris sat patiently as the Scientist explained the options. Even the royal line had flaws. Shan-Lien glanced at her cousin. Though no human subject would dare admit it, the AI could lay out the facts without fearing for its head, wrapping up its presentation with, "So, my lord, it is customary to create a number of possible scions, with the best ones rising to guide civilization." As part of the agreement, Shan-Lien was never to meet any of the other Mothers or their children. She didn't care. Someday he'd be a proud citizen of the Empire, just as she was. Luqas's royal heritage would remain a secret, until the Emperor called for him. But after he was born, she woke many nights with dreams of disaster.

Luqas outstripped other children his age in intelligence, and he was walking and talking in only a few months. Had the price she'd agreed to been worth it, ceding her parental rights to the Empire? Was her baby only a temporary loan? Soon she realized the hard truth. At the top of the space transport stairs, the boy, still only a child, had waved and grinned, eagerly turning to enter the open port. She couldn't blame him, really, for wanting to look for something better. But he was so young… Had he looked back for her? She wasn't sure. She told herself he had.

"I'm so happy to have you here again," Shan-Lien said when they were back in the house. He'd hugged her, but he'd hardly said a word all the way home. Luqas nodded. Older, yes, and more somber than she remembered. Though he appeared in his early teens, he was still her little boy. "Would you like something to eat? I made your favorite strata and potatoes." One advantage of a large empire was co-opting the cuisine of subjugated cultures. They called it assimilating.

"Thanks," Luqas said. "It smells amazing."

Amazing. A word an adult would use.

The dog sniffed Luqas. The kid reached out a hand.

"Do you remember me, boy?" The wagging tail indicated that he might. "What did you name him?"

"I just call him 'Dog,'" Shan-Lien said. "He seems to answer to it."

Luqas laughed and rubbed Dog's wavy golden coat. "Good enough. Where's that strata you talked about?"

They sat across from each other at a table in Shan-Lien's cramped rented flat. She tried not to stare, sizing up the changes since he had left. He wore the gray space corps uniform, only a size or two larger than when he had left twelve years earlier. Between bites, they tried to become re-acquainted.

"Did the mission go all right? Was it dangerous?"

Luqas took a sip of his tea. His hand shook a little. "Everything is classified, Mother."

"Of course, I understand."

"But a lot of what they tell you is inaccurate."

"How do you mean?"

"I mean that most of the children get captured during the missions, or get sold into slavery."

Shan-Lien stifled a gasp. "But you came back all right."

"Yes, the propaganda's just so you don't get your hopes too high and we never come back."

So, the Empire was not all-powerful after all. But she held her tongue. "I only saw a few boys—and one girl. Where were the others? Did they die?"

"The others didn't want to come back."

"Why in heaven's name not? You'd all be welcomed as heroes. Your father would be so proud."

"We're not heroes. And my so-called father has never spoken to me, or taken care of you, for that matter."

Shan-Lien inhaled slowly. She'd heard about returnees having post-traumatic psychological problems. Dog growled softly. They could sense these things. That little gnaw of guilt worked at her stomach. She worried Luqas would be sent on another mission, and she didn't know if she'd be able to stand the endless waiting again. She ladled a spoonful of tomato sauce over the steaming egg dish.

"Let's not talk about it now. Perhaps later, when you feel you'd like to discuss it," she said soothingly.

☯

Shan-Lien tiptoed around the house, careful not to disturb her son. He'd been asleep twenty hours, justly exhausted from his heroic duties on the crusade. She didn't know what those duties were, precisely, but she imagined they'd been strenuous, especially for a youngster. She remembered her shock when Lu Qiang came home from school that day displaying a permission chip on his netlink, begging for her signature. He was still so young. Still, she'd been terrified that she'd be ostracized if she withheld permission. When forced to choose between honor and shame, the choice was obvious. The vids showed parents valiantly offering their children for the expansion effort. Only, they called it a "missionary" effort. A single parent, she had no one to discuss it with, no one to talk her out of it. Luqas had been only eight, a bit chubby, not military material at all. No, not at all. Her teenage son looked almost the same now, his frame still small but well muscled, though his curly, dark hair was streaked with gray. She'd ask him about that later, but for now she'd let him sleep.

"Mother?"

Shan-Lien jumped. The house was always so quiet, she was unused to another voice.

"Did you sleep well?" she asked.

"Very well, thanks," he answered, just like a grown man. A little like his father had been. Excessively formal, until he completed his royal duty and disappeared from her life at the first opportunity.

They had breakfast together, a light repast of grass germ and protein milk. It was the beginning of the holidays celebrating the fall of the Doubters and the rise of the New Empire. "Would you like to go with me to watch the parade?" she asked.

"No, thanks," he replied. "I'm still a little tired. Maybe I'll head back to bed."

"Of course, dear." She was a little worried. Why was he so tired? What had they done to him on that ship? For the first time, she noticed the dark circles under his eyes. She'd overlooked them in her joy to see her son again. As she loaded the bowls into the recleaner, she noticed a slight tremor in his hands.

As if he'd heard her thoughts, he said, "Don't worry, I'm fine. I just need to gather myself back together."

Shan-Lien didn't know what that meant—and she didn't know how it was possible not to worry.

ॐ

Shan-Lien and Lucanus stood on a small hill admiring the procession, staying well back from the military parade streaming by on the boulevard. Luqas had changed his mind about watching, perhaps to please his mother, but he declined to march. Exploding fireworks lit the air, launched from military floaters, as they cleared the way for the returning heroes. A jubilant crowd celebrated the young soldiers and their great achievement in unlocking the secrets of wormhole travel, just in time for the Advent holiday. Shan-Lien had never seen so many women in public at one time. Fully half the people lining the streets, waving colorful banners, and cheering were—female. Many wore long brocade robes with elaborate braided trim on the sleeves and hems. Most of them were not Mothers, however, Shan-Lien noted with satisfaction. She suspected these young women were hoping to catch the eye of one of the soldiers in their gray uniforms. Where *were* all the Mothers? she wondered aloud, but her voice was drowned out in the tumult.

Toward the rear of the parade, a floater carried Emperor Calaneris to the giant temporary stage that had been set up for his address. The sequins on his yellow silk robe threw off sparkling reflections as he mounted the stairs. Raising his hands, he signaled for silence. "My beloved subjects, your divine Emperor has been instructed by his ancestor, the immortal Masquat, to build a residence on a holy new planet, Tian Ming Shen, which will henceforth be known as the Heavenly Seat."

How wonderful, Shan-Lien noted cynically. He's leaving Sheba-4 to fend for itself, just like he did with his family. He had never visited her or Lu Qiang since the day they had met with the designer-AI Scientist. Now he had declared Lucanus some sort of hero but never acknowledged him as his heir. She hated Calaneris, yet she felt awed by the spectacle.

Luqas squeezed his mother's hand, as if hearing her feelings.

"Thanks for changing your mind about the parade," Shan-Lien said. "Having a good time?" She wondered why he had declined to participate in the parade.

"Yes. I wanted one last look."

"What—what do you mean?" she asked. "You aren't leaving again already, are you? You—you've done your duty. And so have I…" She stifled a sob.

"Let's go, Mother," Luqas said. "I have something I want to tell you. I have a plan so we won't ever be separated again. And we can take Dog too."

*****~~~~~*****

Chapter 2.

Quo Vadis?

Luqas felt his thoughts pulsing, a bass note surging in time with his heart. After a nerve-wracking wait for the next local transport, Luqas, Shan-Lien, and Dog headed away from the parade grounds.

"The dog's not allowed," a green-uniformed monitor noted as they boarded. "But, I see you're with a Mother…"

"That's right," Shan-Lien replied with a prim smile. "We need Dog to help me with my balance."

"We are honored, revered Mother," the monitor said with a slight bow. "It's rare to meet a Mother nowadays, since Calaneris banned life extension for you after your role is fulfilled."

Dismayed, Luqas realized he had been lucky to return before his mother died of old age. At least Calaneris's Scientist AI had engineered the emperor's offspring with improved longevity. That explained why Lu Qiang was one of the few children to have been "chosen" and lived to tell the tale.

Luqas exhaled, realizing he'd been holding his breath. His mother was a quick thinker. The car rolled to a stop at the end of the line. Visible in the near distance was an airfield with dozens of parked shuttles.

"Come, Dog," Shan-Lien said, faking a bit of a hobble. She leaned in and whispered, "I wish you'd let me know in advance. We could've avoided all that travel in the wrong direction."

The ship was small but new, a passenger model.

Luqas had outfitted it with barely enough fuel to get them to the rendezvous point he'd set up beyond the end of the sky. He was cutting it close, but utmost secrecy was essential if they were to get away successfully. The people in the royal city of Megali were eager to please their Emperor, and he rewarded snitches handsomely. Best not to attract attention by purchasing large amounts of fuel.

The cabin held two oversize pilot chairs, with room for a third portable seat. Narrow bunks folded up into the walls, to be pulled down during sleep periods. The ship shuddered as it built speed.

"Where are we going, Luqas?" Shan-Lien asked, seating herself in the co-pilot's chair. Luqas wondered if she had flying experience. Her sun-streaked chestnut hair trailed loosely against the high collar of her watered taffeta jacket. Luqas smiled—not as old as she'd let on.

Where are we going? Certainly, a good question at any time. It never hurt to stop and think about where you've been and what path you're on. Luqas didn't answer. He paused to take stock. He knew this much: He knew who he had been—an inconvenient child conveniently conscripted from Sheba-4 to remotely explore the area around the Musquat Empire. But he wasn't a child any more, and he wasn't a member of the empire any longer.

He'd been reunited with his mother, Shan-Lien, former concubine of Calaneris, but he was no better than a bastard, really. Yes, but a royal one, even if he was totally on his own now, without a royal family as safety net. In fact, if they were caught being disloyal, they'd probably be executed on the spot. Unconsciously, Luqas rubbed the back of his neck, recalling a vid he'd seen as a child of a public beheading. The last heartbeat of the condemned had forced a fountain of blood upward, spilling over onto nearby onlookers. A powerful lesson indeed. Luqas'd never met his purported father, only seen a portrait on his mother's wall. Of course, he'd seen many moving, talking, renderings of his father making proclamations. If only they had been of peace instead of war—or domination…. Luqas might not have thought this through completely, but he knew he had to keep moving.

The trip was taking longer than expected. The recirculated air in the cramped cabin had long ago lost its freshness. Luqas consulted the time. They should have arrived at the rendezvous an hour ago. The ship lurched, and a quick glance at the controls showed they were in trouble. Luqas swore. "Look at that."

"What is it?"

"I don't believe it."

"What? Luqas, tell me."

"It's probably our death, Mother. We should be at the portal to the white hole I set up, but I must have miscalculated, and we seem to be in the wrong place at the wrong time."

"Can we go back?"

It wasn't likely. The authorities would soon be sniffing around outside the jump point. The ship had left a big, easy-to-detect, trail of combustion gases leading straight to the portal. And the portal advertised its presence once you knew where to look. Matter bounced noisily in and out, instead of being sucked in and obliterated by the event horizon as with a black hole.

"Is there something I could do to help?" Shan-Lien asked.

"Let me think, would you?" Luqas said, a hint of annoyance cracking his teenage-sounding voice. Most would mistake it for adolescent angst, but he was in his mid-twenties, relatively speaking, the veteran of half a dozen jumps. While the distances were small in terms of the galactic expanse, only a few light-years each, they added up to years in the life of his mother. And he'd spent years traveling in sub-lightspeed time setting up the network of portals. No, it was more like panic.

"I'm sorry for snapping, Mother. We're going weightless, so use your seat ties while I figure this out."

Why wasn't the hole visible? Were they off course? His mouth had gone dry. Suddenly a proximity alarm began to scream. He punched the alarm off.

A faint buzzing sound from his wristband gradually became louder, and he sighed in relief. There it was. The hole just had been practically invisible against the darkness of space. The Masquat toadies wouldn't catch them now.

"Here we go," Luqas said. The sprinkling of remote stars blinked out abruptly, enveloping them in a claustrophobic, pitch-black blanket.

☉

It seemed that only a moment had passed since they entered, but it was a very long moment. When they emerged from the portal, Luqas knew they were several light-years from Sheba-4. He shook away the fog filling his head. Dog barked in agitation, and Shan-Lien called out.

"Luqas!" she cried.

"We made it, Mother."

"We made it?" His mother's eyes mirrored her astonishment. He knew how it looked. How *he* looked. Like an immature kid. Both of them regretted his missed childhood right about now.

He turned on the paragravity and suggested they take a break before the next jump.

"Yes, please," Shan-Lien said. "It was like a nightmare. I don't know why you call it a white hole. It was completely black. Suffocating." She shivered.

Luqas started to chuckle, but then he too shivered. Next time he would pay more attention to time when setting up jumps. He also fretted that the portals he'd created could attract unwanted scrutiny.

"Of course, I said a prayer to Masquat to preserve us," Shan-Lien added. "And I do feel a little more confident, now that I know your little ship will keep us safe. But like I said, I'd appreciate a little advance warning when we're about to try something, um, shall we say, 'out of the ordinary.'"

Quo Vadis?

Luqas knew the search for a home conducive to human life in this vast cosmos was a daunting task. He took heart in the fact that the Empire had discovered quite a few places suitable for conquest. Scanning planets orbiting nearby stars was a good start, but he hoped to settle on a home that would not merely allow life but one with an atmosphere, climate, and gravity that would be closer to what humans might characterize as ideal. In short, a utopia. He'd read a treatise by a philosopher during his long months alone in space, who said hope could be the most powerful thing, or the most useless. Of course, his hope was unrealistic, but there it was.

His mother's religious upbringing in the Masquat Empire had instilled in her a rigid set of values—and entitlements. The religious aristocracy had carte blanche to enforce these standards as they saw fit, and to declare their own actions as proper, moral behavior to be emulated by the masses. Unfortunately, Luqas had missed most of his childhood while traveling the stars, and he didn't believe in the divinity of the emperor. His father was only human, after all. And seeing what the culture had done to his mother did little to warrant his loyalty. Instead of becoming a princess, she'd been used and then cast aside. Enough was enough.

☺

The long years alone had made him strong, independent. But now he had more than himself to think about. If they didn't find a place soon, they'd no longer be Calaneris's dirty little secret.

Between jumps to look for an unclaimed tropical paradise, or even a livable place to start, Luqas began work to program an artificial intelligence that could serve as his right-hand. It would assist him and his mother in speeding up the search for a new home as well as reaching out to others of his people who, like them, were interested in breaking off from the Empire.

What such an AI would entail was fuzzy at first. Luqas knew what he *didn't* want. He didn't want a program that required constant babysitting. That meant designing an ability to learn.

While Luqas pondered how best to mentor the AI intellectually, he delegated most of the everyday scanning and data-crunching to it. No reason a sophisticated enough AI couldn't do both, given enough power and resources. And time. Having time on his hands was what allowed him to perfect his wormhole network. Wormholes obeyed long-held physics equations.

However, given the ship's stripped down circumstances, Luqas didn't yet have the resources to fully deploy the AI design. A new set of math functions was proving useful for machine learning, but its development still had a long way to go. A sticking point seemed to be how to imbue the AI with some sort of moral compass, or at least a philosophy that humans would find acceptable in an artificial ally. One by one, Luqas discarded the Masquat Empire's aspirational principles. Humanity on Sheba-4 had worked very hard to develop their particular morality, which they had solidified into a religious aristocracy. Religion served the upper classes very well, but left others without free will or choice. Luqas was uncertain how to program abilities such as empathy, loyalty, and duty—qualities he called "emotional intelligence." Qualities that even Dog possessed in abundance.

Done right, artificial intelligence could replace the need for religion, though humans had invented many gods over the ages. Luqas didn't have the courage to interfere with his mother's strong faith in the god called Masquat; he recognized the value of giving people something they could believe in. But his mother's god was most assuredly imaginary. Fully implemented, this AI would exist and be seen. It would know that it was a program, but have its own agency. Though it would be part machine, given the ability to not only learn possible solutions to intellectual and physical problems, it would also be part *sophont,* an intelligent, living creature with the ability to judge which solution is best, independent of its human creator, and to perfect its own programming as it saw fit.

Luqas sighed. This AI would have an advantage that no human ever would—knowledge of where it had come from. It would not be just a figment of someone's imagination.

"I will call you AI-M," Luqas said, "for 'Artificial Intelligence/Modulating.'"

After a few more jumps without incident, Luqas decided that the network was functioning well. Each terminus exited near a planet, although most were not habitable by humans. However, many were rich in natural resources and water, which would be useful in supplying a new colony. And they all were beautiful, some sporting fiery lava flows, and others shining with frozen nitrogen glaciers. Shan-Lien noted that she'd grown fond of space travel, much to her son's surprise.

"Don't you want to pick a better name for your AI?" she asked. "It's doing such a good job in charting our course."

"Hmm, I just call it AI-M," he replied, reminding her that she had named her dog, "Dog."

"Well, what about naming this ship, like they do in the Empire?"

"What did you have in mind?" he asked, not succeeding at suppressing a smile.

"I was thinking perhaps 'Can't Remember Where or When.'"

"An excellent choice," Mother.

*****~~~~~*****

Chapter 3.

A Detour

Luqas promised his mother that this would be the last jump. He had only set up five, and that would probably get them a good 18 light-years away from their home system.

The *Can't Remember Where Or When* swam from the darkness into a paler darkness, as their eyes now detected even the slightest bit of what could be called visible.

"It's even emptier than the last place we visited," Shan-Lien grumbled. "Are we ever going to find a new home?" As if sensing her frustration, Dog plopped down at her feet with a low moan and began to scratch at his ears.

AI-M had built a new set of white hole portals, arrayed in his best estimate of the location of a habitable home. This quadrant was dense with middle-aged G-type stars, burning steady and yellow-warm, and similar to the ones Luqas's scouting party'd discovered over the years to harbor life. Four billion years is ample time to try various cocktails of organic soup, provided there was water for the pot. Most would not have intelligent life, but Luqas intended to either find some that did, or settle on a planet that would support them.

"This will just require a bit of patience, I'm afraid," Luqas soothed. They could use more personnel too. He thought about going back the way he came and picking up a few of his former shipmates who, like him, had decided to leave the empire and start independent lives elsewhere.

But to recruit these old comrades, he'd have to risk trespassing on Empire territory, where these deserters hid in the shadows. Officially, they'd gone AWOL, as he too had been when setting up his network. He needed to establish his own home base.

"Patience." Shan-Lien frowned, but then shrugged. "I've got plenty of practice with that."

The AI activated a telescope to track nearby stars for signs of planets, showing up as little black dots traversing the bright solar disks. Luqas glanced at his mother, who seemed engrossed in her game of inventing new, edible foodstuff from the supplies he'd brought along. She told him that a little spice could make an otherwise monotonous life more bearable. He didn't want to mention the possibility that it might take a long time for a planet to make its journey around a sun, depending on its size and orbit. Things could get a lot more monotonous than this…

About two weeks into the trip, Luqas examined the day's telescope data and noted a dark spot in front of one of the nearer stars. He smiled and began to hum as he went through the time lapse.

"Something good?" his mother asked.

"I hope so, Mother. It's a possible planet orbiting that star. See?" He waved her over to look at the output.

"That blotch, you mean?" she asked.

"Well, yes."

"How come it is changing shape?" she asked.

"What?" Luqas bent over to take a closer look. She was right. The planet, if that's what it was, seemed to be losing matter on one side. A bright stripe of green light stretched from pole to pole. That didn't look natural, but it did look like a disaster. How disappointing if they'd caught a planet in the act of disintegrating. That would be just their luck.

Shan-Lien fell back in her seat with a yell. "Luqas!"

Luqas looked up. A third individual—a very tall alien in a white robe—had appeared in the cabin, right beside his mother.

Luqas duplicated her backwards-falling trajectory. Though humanoid, the visitor was a nightmarish caricature of a human. How had it managed to invade their ship, with no warning? Were they about to be destroyed like the planet below?

"Who are you? How did—"

His mind filled with words, all gibberish. The being had telepathic powers. The language sounded calming, however, as if the strange person was trying to communicate good thoughts.

Luqas found his own voice again. "AI-M! Are you there? Can you protect us?"

"Certainly, Creator. What do you need protection from?"

"It's perfectly obvious," Luqas muttered. "This hostile invader."

"Oh, I see there's been a misunderstanding," a voice inside his head said. It was the same voice, but he could understand it now.

AI-M added, "It took a few moments to provide a Sheban dictionary, sorry for the delay. You should be good to go now. The creature's not hostile."

"I apologize for the intrusion," the tall alien said. "My status was rapidly becoming untenable, and I needed a quick exit. Thank you for coming by at the right time. I owe you my life."

Astounded, Luqas stuttered, "You just *materialized* here?"

"Yes, I hope that's not a problem. My name is Benrus. I see this is obviously an inconvenience. I'll just be leaving..." His outline began to blur slightly

"No!" Luqas shouted. "Wait. I mean, yes, please stay. I'm Lucanus—Luqas—and this is my mother, Shan-Lien. We've traveled to your system in search of a new home." He tried hard to stop shaking, but it wasn't working. Damn adrenaline.

"I'm afraid this isn't really a good time," Benrus replied. Luqas thought he detected the hint of amusement in his voice, as his form re-solidfied. The alien was manlike but had no hair—and no mouth. Maybe it was the eyes. Sort of sparkling.

Despite this Benrus creature's polite demeanor, Luqas still wasn't sure what to do. They'd strayed quite far from a wormhole gate, their only avenue of escape.

"We're really not equipped to add another passenger," Luqas said.

"Oh, the third chair is already taken?" Benrus asked, catching Luqas in the lie.

"No, it's just that we have no idea how we could be of help. We don't even know how you got here, much less where to take you."

"We're quite familiar with travel by quantum displacement," Benrus replied. "However, if I hadn't found you quickly, I would have had to retreat into a stasis bubble and hope for rescue."

"Rescue? By whom?"

"That's rather complicated. Our nations have been at war, but my rescuer would have been from the enemy. You see, we're friends." Though he was no expert at interpreting alien body language, Luqas could see that the alien's eyes definitely did not twinkle this time.

"So is your planet disintegrating from this war?" Luqas asked.

"No, this is the war planet, Kantor Prime," Benrus replied. "We're about 20 light-years from our home planet of Jandalat. I'd just like to note that we didn't blow up Kantor Prime," Benrus added. "And the original inhabitants of the war planet are long gone."

Shan-Lien trembled visibly. She turned to her son. "We don't want to get involved in a war zone, Luqas. We've had enough of that where we came from."

"Since the destruction occurring on Kantor Prime, we've declared a suspension to the war," Benrus said. "You are welcome to visit Jandalat, or to continue your journey elsewhere if you wish." The alien gasped slightly. "Oh, is that a dog? We've heard so much about them, their loyalty and devotion to companions. My friend Ralff would love to see one in person."

"Dog's a person," Shan-Lien sniffed. She shook her head at what she took as an obviously foolish statement.

But Luqas quickly heard the siren call of exploration again. A culture advanced enough to conduct its wars on uninhabited planets, far from innocent civilians, seemed practically irresistible. Luqas said, "This is an exciting opportunity, Mother. We can learn about quantum displacement from these people, and we can trade our wormhole technology knowledge."

"I must warn you that politics on Jandalat can be ferocious," Benrus said. "My father holds a high position in our country and is currently brokering a deal, even though he doesn't really trust the enemy. But I'm hoping the distraction of meeting a new space-traveling civilization will lead to a lasting peace."

The three turned at the thumping sound reverberating across the floor. Dog wagged his tail and jumped up on Benrus.

"Oh, all right," Shan-Lien said, "I guess we know the guy's trustworthy—unless he's got treats under that robe of his."

☺

They hardly felt the displacement. But the telescope verified that they were light-years away. Luqas steadied the ship for landing on Jandalat, near Benrus's home city of Peranel. Two gold suns shone in the sky, one much smaller than the other. A grid of silver spires bristled, indicating a large urban population. Benrus directed them toward a paved landing field edged with orange lights.

Shan-Lien asked if the air was breathable.

"I assume so, Mother," Luqas said with a smile. "Benrus was breathing our ship's air on the trip here."

"Our atmosphere is a bit different from yours," Benrus said. "But I was able to easily extract the elements I needed to survive. I believe you should be able to do the same although our physiologies differ. Our denser atmosphere should also do a good job of filtering out harmful ultraviolet radiation."

As they stepped out of the ship, Luqas noted the sky had an orange tinge as well, like a permanent sunset (or was it sunrise?).

Another alien approached the small group. He wore a robe similar to Benrus's, but with a row of flowerlike red embellishments sewn along the hem. A wreath of red flowers completed the outfit.

"Luqas, may I introduce my father, Commander Chobard."

Shan-Lien leaned toward Luqas and whispered, "I hope this isn't another despot like your father."

"We're very pleased to meet you," Luqas said, rather too loudly.

"Welcome to Jandalat," Chobard said. Though he seemed to lack a mouth, the humans could understand him clearly. Luqas resolved to find out later how they were able to communicate via telepathy.

"We are unloading some of your provisions and will take them to your temporary housing," Benrus said. "Once you are settled, we will give you an official welcome. I understand from your mother that you are of royal blood, is that right?"

"Yes, that was true at home, but we no longer observe that," Luqas said. Shan-Lien winced and seemed about to speak, but Luqas aimed a cautioning wave at her.

"I will join you tomorrow for the welcome ceremony," Chobard said. "Benrus will take you to your quarters."

"Thank you," Luqas said. There didn't seem to be any sort of handshaking or bowing, he observed with relief. Less chance of putting his foot in his mouth. He was also glad he wouldn't have to eat strange food and display what would undoubtedly be taken as poor table manners at a banquet. Aloud, he said, "Isn't that nice, Mother? A welcoming ceremony." They walked only a short distance to a windowless tower at the edge of the landing field.

"I'm sorry to have to quarantine you here overnight, but there was some concern that you might carry pathogens that would be inimical to our people," Benrus said.

"Perfectly understandable," Luqas said. "We always took rather drastic measures to avoid contamination when making first contacts with alien species. This time *we're* the aliens."

Benrus showed them into a room with rather plain furnishings. It was large, but only had a pair of platforms that would serve as couches or beds. Flat panels lined the walls. A doorway led to a small bathroom and toilet.

Shan-Lien surveyed the quarters. "Well, it's no worse than where I used to live," she said.

"Feel free to sample the entertainment and news. If you need anything, please just speak up. I'm quarantining too. I'll be listening next door."

"So, no privacy, eh," Shan-Lien said. "Also no different from where I used to live."

"I'm sorry," Benrus said again. "But I did warn you that we are still at war. Hopefully that will be over soon." He exited and closed the door softly behind him.

"How do you suppose they eat and drink?" Shan-Lien said.

"Careful, Mother, he can probably hear us." In truth, he wondered the same thing. Without a course in Jandalan anatomy, he could only speculate. Luckily they'd been assured there would be no alien dissections tonight.

೨

Shan-Lien awoke first, as yellowish light seeped in behind her eyelids and pinged her retinas. The walls seemed to be glowing, perhaps a way of signaling the new day. She rose and headed to the tiny bathroom to relieve herself. The toilet didn't have a handle, but her emiction seemed to disappear as soon as it hit the bottom. She grunted and returned to find Luqas sitting on the edge of his platform talking to the air.

"Good morning, I think," she said. A tray with cups of tea and warm bowls of cereal sat on the edge of the platform.

They heard a knock.

"That smells good," Benrus said.

"Oh, you can smell, then."

"Of course," he replied.

"I don't suppose you'd like a cup of tea?" Shan-Lien said.

"Yes, thanks, that sounds lovely," he said. Shan-Lien scurried off to find another cup, curiosity burning about how the tall alien would drink it without a mouth. Another cup blinked into existence alongside the other two.

Nonplussed, Shan-Lien said, "Well, here you are, then." She set the cup on the platform. "I'm afraid I have no idea what kind it is."

To her surprise, a shallow slit opened in Benrus's face, and he poured the whole cup in at once. The slit closed without a trace.

"Mm, delicious. It's nice that you have liquidized foods," Benrus said. "Otherwise, we would have to use digestive enzymes to process the meal into slime so that we can suck nutrition out."

Both Shan-Lien and Luqas stood there with their mouths open, speechless for a moment. Luqas took a sip. "Yes, quite good. Thanks, Mother." *When in Jandalat...*

At the sound of a short musical beep, Benrus announced that his father Chobard sought admittance, which Shan-Lien and Luqas quickly granted.

"Having found no extraplanetary microbes that we would find harmful, we welcome you to move freely here in Peranel, with an escort, of course. I'm here to accompany you to the welcoming ceremony later this morning. But would you like to take a short tour first? I have something that you might find of interest in our textile factory."

The group followed Chobard to an open-air structure, where trays lined with paper held sprigs of leaves. Looking more closely, they saw thousands of wriggling worms chewing on the leaves. Shan-Lien jumped back with a slight squeal.

Chobard pointed. "This is where we manufacture silk, one of the most prized fabrics. When you landed, I noticed that you wore a ceremonial red sash. Is that the royalty designation that Benrus told me about?"

"Well, not exactly," Shan-Lien said. "It means that I am a Mother."

"Ah, yes, we're quite familiar with human reproduction. You are a female, then."

Shan-Lien snorted. "Of course."

"When we visited a human planet in the past, we admired a fabric called silk, which is produced from the cocoons of a creature called a moth. We found a way to separate the moths from the cocoons without killing them. Once these larvae reach full growth, they will spin cocoons made of silk. The robe I'm wearing is made of it."

"It does rather shimmer," Shan-Lien said, reaching out to touch Chobard's sleeve. Suddenly shy, she quickly removed her hand.

"Silk fiber has a prismlike structure, so it refracts incoming light at different angles. It is really quite durable and can be colored to match your sash. I believe it would make a suitable fabric for your official State clothing, if you are interested. Oh, and would your son like a sash made of silk as well?"

"No, thanks," Luqas said. "We males don't wear them, since we don't bear young."

"Oh, I see," Chobard said. "We Jandalans are hermaphroditic, so the honor of parenthood is what you might call interchangeable."

"Thanks, Chobard," Shan-Lien said. "I'd love to wear a shawl made of your silk."

"I'll order that right away," he replied. "And now, let's head over to the military headquarters for the ceremony. There won't be much to it, but I know our people will be glad to know that my young son has brought us a new ally in the war."

"A war that we hope will end soon," Benrus added. He described the destruction he'd seen of Kantor Prime. He'd had hardly enough time to displace into space before the whole war planet disintegrated. He was glad his friend Ralff had left the week before, but he'd explain that later. For now, the important part was that the home planet was in danger as well. A unified front was imperative.

*****~~~~~*****

Chapter 4.

War Zone

The war wasn't over in a day. In fact, it dragged on another year. Jandalat's summer season had come and gone, the vermilion skies turning a pale shade of pink as frost-laden air circled the Northern hemisphere in gently whirling vortexes.

Benrus repeatedly pleaded with his father to allow a delegation from the Southern continent to state their terms. But after Benrus told his father about the enemy he'd become close friends with on Kantor Prime, the old one's attitude hardened. "We can't allow spies to ingratiate themselves and turn us into quislings," he said.

In some ways, Luqas agreed with the elder Jandalan. His own father was notorious for using spies and assassins against enemies of the Empire, including the genetically enhanced Gonsha women, witches who could either influence or poison susceptible minds.

Luqas sensed that Shan-Lien grew more irritated with his extended "stopover" on Jandalat. "When are we going to get out of here and look for a permanent home?" she asked, with increasing regularity. At least she had stopped asking where they were going, for which Luqas was grateful, because he still didn't know. He was so busy learning about Jandalat that he had made little further progress on the AI. Lately, it was mostly in sleep mode, unless Shan-Lien asked for its help.

Luqas looked up to see Shan-Lien entering the hall.

"Join us, Mother," he called. "How is it going with the new house?" Benrus had obtained a whole floor of a nearby residential tower for them to furnish as they saw fit, and Shan-Lien had thrown herself into the project whole-heartedly.

"The living space is quite comfortable, Luqas, and the security fencing we borrowed from the ship is operating well, but I'm worried that we are running out of the basic supplies we brought from Sheba-4," she said. "The enzymes for the longevity drug are also in short supply, and the analyzer is complaining that we won't be able to make any soon. Without it I won't even make it to a hundred."

"I'm afraid that's my fault," Benrus said. "I never asked what your expected life spans are. I just assumed you were quite young, especially you, Luqas, being the smaller human."

Luqas glanced at his mother. "It's not your fault, Benrus. I was genetically modified as a child so that I would age slowly and travel in cramped quarters, while my mother, being an ordinary citizen, had to take supplements to temporarily head off aging."

"Nonetheless," Benrus said, "I gave you to believe that the quantum travel ban would be over quite soon, and I've delayed you from proceeding with your journey. Let me think about how we can best correct the situation."

☺

The following day Luqas and his mother invited Benrus to their grand new apartment.

"Tea?" Shan-Lien asked.

"Oh, yes, please."

As they sat drinking tea and sampling Shan-Lien's signature afternoon pastry, the Jandalan made his tea disappear in a decidedly nonstandard way.

Luqas asked, "Before the war, where was your favorite place to visit? How exciting to travel to another planet on just the power of your own mind. Perhaps you could teach me how to travel in that way."

"How very diplomatic of you to couch your request in those terms," Benrus replied. "All citizens are skilled at quantum displacement, but the places they choose to visit vary greatly. It is true that my home city is utilitarian, some might say, ordinary. My favorite place isn't so far as you might think," Benrus replied. "I love the mountainous region near my friend Ralff's city in Southern. The architecture is beautiful, and the Place of Contemplation park is famous throughout this region of the galaxy. It is where the art of displacement was discovered and contains examples of the different civilizations known to Jandalat, as well as an advanced quantum computing facility. We could jump there easily, but my father does not permit it."

Benrus shared some stories about the old days, when Jandalat had a world government. Travel was considered an inalienable right, with citizens of both hemispheres passing freely on business and vacation. The Southern hemisphere was known for warmer temperatures, high culture, and scientific advancement, while the Northern was a center of military achievement and discipline. Over time, that cooperation had soured and turned to distrust. The bustling headquarters that Benrus and Chobard inhabited was a perfect example of Northern culture. News feeds on every wall spewed a constant barrage of information to keep everyone up to the minute on events and strategies.

"You know, I feel the tea ceremony that you have so kindly shared with me the past several months, has given me an idea about how to address your nutrient supply problem."

"Yes, Benrus?" Luqas scooted forward, perching like a bird about to launch into flight.

"But I have to warn you that it might be dangerous."

"Well, let us hear it anyway," Shan-Lien said.

"We can go to Southern and talk to my friend."

"You mean this Ralff person, the one your father forbids you to see?"

"Exactly. Of course, Father can't really prevent it."

"I don't know…" Shan-Lien said.

"What could Ralff do to help with the supplies?" Luqas said.

"He's one of the foremost Southern experts on biochemical research, and he's been more places than anyone on the planet. Perhaps one of the destinations set up in the Place of Contemplation would prove a source of the chemicals you need."

Shan-Lien asked why it would be dangerous.

"It could be considered fraternizing with the enemy. If caught, we could all be executed," Benrus said.

"I'm willing to risk it, if you are," Luqas said.

"We will need to train you to apply displacement, and it will have to be in secret," Benrus said.

"I want to come too," Shan-Lien added. "AI-M can look after Dog for a bit, right?"

"I suppose so," Luqas said, "but it's not Dog I'm worried about. It's that AI-M hasn't been trained to tend to pets. Besides, I intended to personally get closer with Dog after all that time away. If you could make up a list of the duties of a pet owner, I think that would be helpful."

"I get it," Shan-Lien said. "Like the instructions you give a babysitter when you leave for the evening. Of course, I never could afford one for you."

☙

As the team blinked away, one by one, AI-M skimmed the instructions Shan-Lien had left. From what it could tell, the main task was to make sure the animal wasn't dead upon the travelers' return. That should be relatively easy, assuming they weren't gone so long that the dog died of old age. The pet came from the same planet as Luqas and Shan-Lien, so AI-M assumed it would be able to breathe the same air and eat the same food.

Correction: Upon closer reading, the food was different from human food.

Step 1: Feed Dog a cup of dry kibble twice a day.

Hmm, this might require a bit of research. AI-M had watched Dog gobble his breakfast from a bowl every day, but had paid little attention to what exactly he was eating. What and where was kibble? A hurried search of the ship's knowledge library yielded a recipe for kibble that claimed to be suitable for dogs, although there was disagreement as to the best formulation to maintain health. AI-M prepared several different compounds and thought it best to test them on Dog to see which the animal preferred. Apparently, Dog preferred them all, devouring each one quickly. Only the last formula seemed to disagree with the dog, which it regurgitated onto the floor.

AI-M embodied its avatar and moved to clean up the moist mess of kibble, but Dog growled. Though the dog could not speak in human language, it was clearly displeased. AI-M briefly considered what action to take, and in that brief timespan, Dog reconsumed the kibble. This time, the kibble seemed to stay inside the dog.

Step 2: Walk Dog twice a day, after meals.

"Where would you like to walk, Dog?" AI-M inquired. There was no answer, though the dog wagged its tail expectantly. AI-M decided to wait a while to let the dog choose a route for its walk. Nothing seemed to happen, except that Dog grew increasingly agitated. Finally, it turned around to face the north and relieved itself on the rug.

It was unclear how much excrement to expect. AI-M's avatar bent to the pile and incinerated it, leaving a small burn hole on the rug. The AI deduced that "walk the dog" was an expression meaning, "find a place *outside* for the dog to relieve itself."

Unfortunately Shan-Lien hadn't supplied further details about how long this walk should take, or how far outside it should be. Dog seemed eager to go outside, and equally eager to go back inside.

Step 3: Brush Dog daily. Also, brush his teeth.

This assignment was proving unexpectedly time-consuming. The AI's multitasking skills had grown rusty while on quiet mode during the humans' visit to the planet Jandalat. AI-M consulted the knowledge library again on proper care of pets, beyond simply the manufacture of kibble. There were whole *volumes* of information on training dogs how not to poop on the carpet, using collars and leashes for walking, and so forth. Additionally, it was important to provide fresh water with every meal. The water was excreted as urine, and that activity was not suitable for indoors, either. What was Shan-Lien thinking? She was lucky to have not killed the animal with her lackadaisical methodologies, and it appeared that Dog was training her, not the other way around.

In the evening, ignoring all of AI-M's attempts at communication, Dog turned up his nose at dinner and howled. AI-M realized that Dog evidently missed its humans, and the avatar reached out to gently stroke the top of its narrow skull. Was this realization what was meant by empathy? That was a matter for further study. Meanwhile, AI-M resolved to use proven artificial intelligence techniques to design a much more rigorous training set for the semi-sentient creature. Luqas was sure to be pleased with Dog's progress when he returned.

☙

As promised, Southern's capital city was indeed quite different from Benrus's home town, like a place straight out of a storyvid. Sedate, Art Deco buildings lined wide, curving boulevards, and a range of steep, white-capped mountains jutted splendidly to create a glittering backdrop. Led by Benrus, the trio of supplicants passed behind the Monastery of Contemplation located a short walk from the city. A deserted path wound up into the foothills and behind a tree-shrouded grove, where a columned marble building stood. The twitter of birds lent a happy sound. The area brought back memories of the warm, sunny neighborhood Luqas had grown up in on Sheba-4.

"Ben!" An alien, practically a twin to Benrus, only a few inches shorter appeared and approached them with open arms.

Luqas and Shan-Lien averted their eyes discreetly, while the two aliens embraced.

"May I introduce my friend, Ralff," Benrus said. "These are the humans I told you about, Luqas and Shan-Lien."

"I'm very pleased to meet you," Ralff said. "I've been to Earth many times, and I'm quite fond of the cultures and scenery there."

"Earth?" Shan-Lien said. "I've never heard of it."

"Oh, I just assumed… Earth is a fascinating planet," Ralff said. "It's the cradle of humanity, before it scattered around the galaxy, but its civilizations have risen and fallen numerous times over the millennia. Your people are quite volatile." He turned to Benrus. "Although I admit we've had a spate of wars here on Jandalat as well. Some say human culture has infected us. I personally think the opposite. Benrus tells me you're looking to manufacture a particular protein that's not common on Jandalat?"

"Yes, either that, or a way to genetically treat my mother to reduce her mortality rate," Luqas said. "You see, I was given gene therapy at birth to make me less vulnerable to radiation and to lengthen my life span so that I could travel in space. Mother doesn't have those genes."

"Ah, yes, many of the original human descendants are short-lived," Ralff observed. "I don't see why it wouldn't be possible to deconstruct a sample of your DNA and insert some of your genetic mapping into your mother's. Failing that, we could inject proteins into your mother's brain that would inhibit neural activity and activate transcription factors that would extend her probable lifespan. Let's go inside."

Ralff led the group into the marble entrance of the Place of Contemplation.

"Why is it called that?" Shan-Lien asked.

"A few thousand years ago, an ancestor named Gant'er hiked to this spot and found himself in an entirely different environment. The scenery had changed completely, from forest to a grass-covered meadow. It turned out to be a place called Earth. Gant'er approached the animals grazing there, knowing them to be harmless, when a shepherd approached him, waving a staff. Worried, he pulled his robe across his face and stumbled backward. That was when he found himself back home, with the Monastery hunkering below. It was our people's first experience of quantum displacement.

"Our people immediately began traveling all over the known universe, and we experienced a blossoming of knowledge, tapping the cosmos for new discoveries. Our most recent work has been in developing a quantum computer and power sources, which might enable us to build new habitats for our people. As for Earth, we even sent a few missions to learn more about the humans there, being careful not to disturb the status quo like we had accidentally done with the shepherd. Everyone was especially taken with your horses. Beautiful four-legged creatures. We had nothing like them on Jandalat."

"Horses, eh?" Shan-Lien said. "Never heard of them. What's wrong with Dog? He's got four legs."

"We love dogs as well," Ralff said.

Mollified, Shan-Lien said, "yes, Dog's a very good boy."

"I love it when you tell that story," Benrus said. "It gets me every time. I hope someday we'll get back to that goal."

Weeks passed, while Ralff worked to perfect the genetic mods for Shan-Lien. Luqas asked for lab space where he could work on artificial intelligence improvements to tweak the wormhole technology.

"I'm sorry we haven't had time to teach you to displace yet," Benrus apologized. "I've felt it best to accompany you on these place-altering jumps. We wouldn't want to leave you stranded in a place with no exit. Luck has a way of being unpredictable to the uninitiated."

"No problem, Benrus," Luqas said. "We've been very lucky so far. Mother's treatments have gone well, and she reports no adverse effects, except, of course, that nothing ever happens fast enough for her. Now she's talking about genetically modifying Dog as well."

Benrus made daily trips back to Peranel. He had succeeded in keeping his work with Ralff secret, until he forgot to change the outfit he'd worn on the latest trip with Luqas. The two Jandalans looked nearly identical in the Southern uniforms, although Benrus was a little taller.

"What is the meaning of this?" Chobard demanded. "Why are you wearing a Southern uniform?" Benrus blinked and disappeared back to Ralff's laboratory.

"We've been discovered," Benrus said. "Of course it's my fault again. I wore the wrong clothes home, and now my father knows something is afoot. I expect him any min—"

Chobard materialized abruptly, interrupting in mid-sentence.

"I asked you a question, Benrus."

"I'm sorry, Father, but this was the only way. Our guests needed Ralff's expertise to get them on their way."

More aliens suddenly appeared, gathering close to Chobard. Luqas counted at least seven. Their robes were decorated along the hems, like Benrus's. Northern soldiers, or else Chobard's bodyguards.

"Your orders, sir?" one said.

"Hold until I give the order," Chobard said. "Keep an eye on the Southerner." He cleared a path forward and leaned in close to his son. "What exactly is your plan? This could be considered treason if you are aiding the enemy."

"It's not treason, Father," Ben replied. "You know that Ralff is a scientist. We're consulting with him on improvements to the human genetic code to enable Luqas's mother to live longer. That's all, I promise."

Luqas could swear that Chobard's eye color darkened. He didn't see any weapons being brandished about, but on the other hand, he had no idea what kind of weapons the Southern soldiers might carry under their robes.

"Ralff, you must come with us. When I hear your arguments, I'll decide whether I believe you, or whether I should arrest you and Benrus," Chobard said.

"I'll come willingly and explain everything," Ralff said.

🌀

All four "co-conspirators" found themselves in the Northern prison complex. A room had been prepared for interrogating the suspects, and the young Jandalans had agreed not to disapparate.

"As Benrus told you," Ralff said, "the human woman has a rather primitive brain chemistry that only allows a life span of about 100 years, due to breakdown of protein signaling components. I've been working on creating some scaffolding proteins to help bind a protein kinase to substrate proteins in her brain. The kinase would inhibit glutamine and damp down extra activity that is a hallmark of the aging brain, thus regulating the pace at which aging occurs."

Chobard nodded. "That is impressive work. Would this help our own people live longer as well?"

"Undoubtedly, sir. We are not that different from humans biologically, although we already outlive humans such as Shan-Lien fourfold, due to the work done centuries ago on gene modifications via CRISPr. Those mods were inheritable, so all Jandalans now carry those genes. This new technique would just be an add-on that could be applied to individuals."

Chobard asked, "What sort of enhancement are we talking about?"

"Probably another doubling of lifespan, though not directly inheritable."

"Would you be willing to share this technology?"

"Of course," Ralff and Benrus said simultaneously, each crossing their hands over chests in the Jandalan sign of assent. Ralff chuckled.

"All right. We will release you, and I will resume the talks with Southern. We have been at war too long, and it's time to share in the benefits of our latest technological achievements. This is no time for petty jealousy," Chobard said.

Luqas smiled. Chobard appeared to have a heart under that robe, after all. As they left the prison Luqas whispered to Benrus. "Nicely put. Your father's a consummate politician."

⊙

That evening Chobard appeared at Benrus's quarters in Peranel. "I see that Ralff has apparently moved in. You're a couple, then."

Benrus was surprised by his father's sudden about-face. He wondered what had finally convinced his father and showed Chobard to a seat. "May I offer you a cup of tea?" he asked.

"What?" Chobard said. "No, thanks." Turning to Ralff, he said, "I wanted to continue our discussion earlier today. Although our human guests are obviously inferior, I didn't want to seem ungracious by seeming eager for them to be on their way. But in truth, I *am* eager, because we are facing some serious existential issues that we need your help with."

Chobard called up a holographic image of the war planet. It was disintegrating rapidly, torn apart by high-energy green lightning. Fountains of steam and rivers of lava crept across what remained of the landscape.

His father had been listening to his reports after all. Benrus nodded. "Yes, we were lucky to evacuate Kantor Prime, or we'd be dead, right, Ralff?"

Ralff studied the image. "I evacuated earlier than you, Ben, when our troops were withdrawn. I hadn't realized it had gotten so bad. Then I got caught up in the much more interesting search for a longevity drug…"

Chobard waved to silence Ralff. "It is spreading. We just received word that the quantum computing facility at the Place of Contemplation has been destroyed. And several of our normal evacuation avenues have disappeared."

Benrus jumped up, exclaiming, "Here on Jandalat? That's incredible."

Ralff added, "I agree. We were just there, explaining how the Monastery is the birthplace of our history of space explorations. It is as if someone has tried to cut us off from our dimensional travel ability."

"I believe your analysis is correct," Chobard said. "And it appears to have come from outside Jandalat. Can you help us defend against another incursion? It could destroy our whole planet, like it did to Kantor Prime."

Ralff said, "We'll go look at the damage in person right away." He gestured to Benrus, who was already on his feet."

"Hurry," Chobard said. "This is urgent."

"Yes, Father," Benrus said, as the two hurried out into the night. A greenish light was bleeding upward into the normally dark orange sky, leaving a brown stain across the horizon.

Rather than hike up to the destroyed Monastery grounds, they boarded scooters to reach the trail leading to the Place of Contemplation, but when they neared the grove of trees where it should be, the forest was ablaze. Jagged forks of green lightning struck the area repeatedly, setting fire to an increasingly large perimeter. Their attempt to record the event ended abruptly, as Benrus realized they couldn't reach the Place of Contemplation. He pulled his comm device from his robe and called his father. "We're heading home, but we can't displace. We're going to have to take the long way back."

"Good," Chobard said. "We'll try to monitor remotely. Be careful."

Ben and Ralff turned, but another bolt of green lightning struck behind them, cutting off their retreat. Only a narrow strip of land remained between the Place and the new conflagration. Their scooters were unreachable. As they ran, Ralff tripped and fell, ripping his robe and bloodying his hand. His facial slit opened, sucked the blood away, and sealed shut again.

"Keep going!" Benrus urged. They fled, crashing through the surrounding brush looking for another way down to the city.

"We've got to warn Father that a stasis pod is in order," Benrus said. "With no dimensional avenues available, people will have to wait it out."

"There's no way we can shelter the whole population that way," Ralff said. "We've got to warn Luqas and Shan-Lien too."

"No time!" Ben said, preparing a stasis pod. "Ready?"

Ben and Ralff held hands and stepped inside, taking their last look at the planet of Jandalat.

*****~~~~~*****

Chapter 5.

Fire Run With Me

Luqas and Shan-Lien watched tensely as Chobard spoke to his staff rapidly in a dialect they couldn't understand.

"Wait, slow down," Shan-Lien said. "What's happening? Are Ben and Ralff coming back?"

Chobard's eyes had turned dark, a bad sign.

"We fear they are lost," he replied. "There is a disruption in the normal universe we are used to, I'm afraid. It is like the one we saw earlier on Kantor Prime. It's even worse than a simple planetary disaster. Our astronomers have reported that nearby stars are winking out."

"Are we in danger?" Shan-Lien asked. No one answered. "Luqas?"

"What about your dimensional shifting abilities?" Luqas asked Chobard.

"Without our power supplies, we have a limited ability to escape," Chobard said. "I am putting our family into a stasis pod. You are welcome to join us if you want."

"That's extremely generous of you," Luqas said.

"Perhaps not," Chobard said. "Once inside stasis, we are unaware of the passage of time. Without others of our people to end the stasis, it's possible we could remain until the end of the universe."

Shan-Lien gripped Luqas's arm.

"Then I think we will take our chances and follow the wormholes out to another area of the galaxy," Luqas said. "I don't have any idea where we'll end up, but at least it will be quick, and it'll get us away from here."

"Very well," Chobard said, turning to his fellow Jandalans and issuing what Luqas took to be emergency orders to go into stasis.

"Wait," Shan-Lien said. "We have room for one more, and we owe you, Chobard. Come with us."

"I'd feel like a traitor…" Chobard began.

"Someone's got to be left to find your people in stasis and get them out," Luqas said. "Mother's right. Come with us."

Chobard crossed his arms over his chest. He barked an order, and watched as a dozen coruscating globes appeared and his people leaped inside. He turned to Luqas, and said, "Your ship is in storage nearby."

As he said this, the curtain of green lightning sliced through the ceiling of the military headquarters war room. Luqas, Chobard, and Shan-Lien fled to the airfield hangar. They dived through the hatch of the ship and Luqas yelled, "AI-M! Take us out of here!" He only prayed the AI knew what he meant by that.

☺

Apparently AI-M had a well-developed sense of self-preservation, because they emerged from a wormhole journey alive and only a bit the worse for wear.

"Oh, I really hate those worm jumps," Shan-Lien said. "It feels like your insides are being turned out."

"I'm amazed that we escaped," Chobard said. "Did you know where we were headed?"

"Not really, but it's probably a known system," Luqas replied. "AI-M chose it." He only knew it was probably one of the worm jumps he'd set up earlier, when he was planning to gather his mother from Sheba-4 and defect from the Masquat Empire. But in the past, he'd always set up jumps himself. He couldn't vouch for what AI-M had taken as his orders—"Get us out of here" was not very specific. He would address AI-M again, this time asking where the hell this pseudo-displacement had taken them.

"We are near the edge of the galactic perimeter," AI-M said. "I felt it safest to displace as far as possible from the threat."

Luqas whistled. "Sheba-4 orbits a yellow star near the galactic center. I find it incredible that we've managed to travel such a huge distance." A thought struck him.

"Are we still in the same relative time? We're not about to enjoy the heat death of the universe, are we?"

"No," AI-M replied, supplying little detail.

Shan-Lien looked into the air, as if she could see the location of the invisible AI voice. "What about a planet called Tian Ming Shen?" she asked. "That's where your father is," she added, nodding to Luqas.

"That is farther from the galactic center than we are now," the AI responded. "Although there appears to have been incursions in the vicinity of Tian Ming Shen, besides Jandalat."

"So we're safe here?" Shan-Lien asked.

"For the time being."

"I think AI-M's right," Luqas said. "We're only safe 'for the time being.' By being at the edge of the known galaxy, we are sitting in a sparse area. The stars here are spread out by tremendous distances. Hopefully it'll give us a breather, while we assess what's been happening."

"What's the plan, then?" Chobard asked. "Start jumping all the way back?"

Luqas thought about it for what seemed like an eternity to his passengers. Finally, he spoke.

"We're not going back yet. I want to study the incursions. I need to work with AI-M to gather the data we need to see if we can save what's left of the affected area. I suspect it's some sort of attack by a malevolent civilization, something far worse than the Masquat Empire's territorial acquisition. Plus, that green lightning weapon is like nothing I've ever heard of."

"What are we going to eat while you study this thing?" Shan-Lien asked. "We were running low on supplies even back on Jandalat."

"You're right, Mother," Luqas said. "I have to admit that you're the sensible one around here, always asking whether something's feasible or not."

"Well, you're the boy with the big ideas," Shan-Lien said with a smile. "Like I said before, you had me at 'we can bring the dog.'"

"Though I have no pet companionship to offer, I'll add whatever expertise I have in quantum displacement," Chobard said. "It'll either be a pioneering experiment like that of Gant'er, or a grand illusion gone bad. We Jandalans have always sought knowledge, and it has always brought us prosperity."

Luqas thanked the two older people for putting up with his admittedly sketchy plan. But his new partnership with AI-M encouraged him to keep exploring, even if it seemed they might risk death by opposing this unknown incursion. "It's important to start monitoring right away," Luqas said, "in case we find we have to make a hasty exit."

"I'd dearly like to sleep in a bed instead of a seat," Shan-Lien replied. "But I suppose there are priorities." Luqas pursed his lips and said nothing. Everyone wished for additional living space beyond the cramped quarters of Luqas's small ship. Upon retiring he dreamed about how his mother had showed him vids as a child about space heroes exploring the universe in giant ships, and then tucked him into bed.

When he awoke, Luqas rolled out of his bunk and gasped in surprise. An addition had appeared outside, dwarfing the tiny spaceship and connected by a tunnel to three pressurized rooms. The floors were covered with low-pile industrial carpet, and each room was furnished with a platform bed and small bathing room. A fourth room, much larger than the others, was empty.

He hadn't designed these. They were like the bedroom he remembered from home.

"AI-M, did you do this?"

"I'm not sure what you're referring to," the AI replied.

"This isn't possible! You manufactured all of this out of whole cloth? Where did you get the materials?"

"The universe contains an abundance of raw materials."

"I see," Luqas said, slowly, although he really didn't understand. "Well, thank you. Mother's going to be really pleased."

"You're welcome, Luqas."

Luqas grimaced. So much for the emotional intelligence part of this creation.

"Perhaps you could give me a demo of how you imported enough materials to build an entire habitat." *Not to mention how the AI had mastered putting them together in space.*

"Certainly," AI-M replied. "Please follow me to the cargo bay." That explained the fourth room's purpose. "Perhaps you should stand back a little, while I construct a transporter." Luqas retreated, until his back bumped against the opposite wall. AI-M manifested a large, translucent globe, about ten feet in diameter. Its jellylike surface began to shimmer, and the skin turned transparent. Dark objects began to fill the rotating globe. When it had become nearly full, Luqas heard a clunk, as the globe stopped receiving solid matter. A port opened in the lower half, and some of the material spilled out onto the floor. It appeared to be chunks of a gray mineral ore, perhaps quartz.

"How does it work?" Luqas asked in wonder.

"I got the idea from the Jandalans' stasis bubble, although it is impossible to open their invention from the outside. This transporter, as I call it, is simply a way to carry more matter through a wormhole."

"What is the substance being transported?"

"It's called riprap, human-placed rubble dumped along shorelines to prevent flooding. There was quite a quantity of it outside a city on a human planet that is largely ocean. Highways and buildings made of an aggregate called concrete had been demolished to make way for future improvements, and I surmised that the debris wouldn't be missed."

"Oh, that's a good idea. You're actually helping clean up a garbage problem," Luqas said with a smile. "I don't suppose that planet would be suitable for us?"

"Unlikely. There are billions of humans there already. However, Chobard has visited it already, so you might ask him for his opinion."

Once again, Luqas was surprised by the AI's apparent humility in asking for a second opinion.

"How did you know Chobard had been there?"

"I have many free cycles, during which I can scan the Jandalan's dream state. The place he visited was called Earth."

"Did you scan my dreams too?" Luqas asked. His initial delight at the AI's initiative had turned to nervousness. He didn't know whether to approve whole-heartedly, or to simply deem the question moot for now.

The AI answered in the affirmative.

"Ah well, perhaps we ought not to speak of this to Chobard just yet," Luqas said.

"Of course, as you wish, Luqas," AI-M replied.

Luqas approached the slowly collapsing gelatinous globe. When he poked a finger onto the surface, it dissolved with a pop. Not too different from popping soap bubbles when he was a boy…

Luqas heard Shan-Lien clear her throat as she entered the recently attached cargo room. In his amazement at the recent miracle, he hadn't heard her footsteps, or the toenails of Dog clattering on the metal floors.

"How much did you hear, Mother?" Luqas asked.

"Not enough to understand what's going on here," she replied. "What's all this debris? Have we hit something? Wait, have you added a door? How exciting. Where does it lead?" She started to walk toward the door.

"Wait, I'm not sure it's safe yet. AI-M is still building it."

Shan-Lien shook her head. "I can't believe your AI built all this, just by looking at our dreams."

So, his mother *had* heard pretty much everything. "Yes, that seems to be the case, at least in part."

"Well, if that's so, why hasn't it found the planet of our dreams yet? It'd be nice to see blue sky again for a change—oh, no offense, Chobard."

The Jandalan had just walked in. The scene of surprise, wonder, and questioning repeated itself throughout the remainder of the day.

◕

Luqas inspected the habitat carefully, testing whether the air pressure and temperatures were suitable for his "crew," and suggesting amenities to the AI. The next day, bathtubs had been added to the each of the quarters. Finally, he declared the addition habitable, and they all moved into their own rooms.

Sitting in a tub of fragrant, steaming water that night, Luqas tried to relax. The humidity was appreciated after the weeks of dry, filtered air had parched all of their lungs. He could feel his hair curling, an odd but welcome sensation. "I bet I've lost a half kilo of dirt," he said aloud.

"Only a small quantity of dirt," a disembodied voice announced. "Most of the excess consisted of skin cells and skin-living microorganisms." A low-pitched vacuuming sound hummed as the water drained. "Do you want me to preserve the organic material for recycling?"

Luqas pressed his lips together. "Thanks, that won't be necessary," he said, as tactfully as possible, considering he was speaking to an AI. He was going to have to fine-tune the wireless intercom, not to mention the bathroom's functions. Grooming should be a simple process, not a conversation with an eavesdropping automaton.

The next two weeks passed uneventfully, as they performed more analysis jumps. No more incidents with the green lightning had occurred in the vicinity of the wormholes. At dinner, Shan-Lien waxed rhapsodic about the new quarters.

"Do you notice anything different about me?" she asked. "I've got a new haircut, and look at the polish on my nails. Do you like the color? I think the red suits me."

"Very nice, Mother," Luqas mumbled, taking a very large bite of some sort of stringy mashed vegetable which she had declared her latest "specialty." He chewed for a long time, before chugging down a full tankard of mild beer.

He spent the rest of the evening poring through the latest area scans, but nothing looked perfect as a permanent refuge. As he prepared for sleep, he tossed and turned but couldn't drift off. He finally realized what had been bothering him about the recent space ship "improvements." This place was getting too comfortable. He was beginning to feel like a prisoner in his own creation. Well, not exactly a prisoner. But his recent exploratory phase had ground to a confining halt. He had to get out of there. It was time to move on.

*****~~~~~*****

Chapter 6.

Wanderers

Luqas fought the urge to point the ship anywhere—any direction—anything to get away from the tedium of "camping out" at the edge of the quadrant with nothing to do.

He stared at the graphic display that summarized the latest survey. Same as ever. No, wait, there was a blinking light alongside the display, indicating a possible find. He scooted forward, his pulse picking up slightly.

"Dog! You'll get hair all over Luqas!" Shan-Lien yelled at the companion that had taken up residence at Luqas's feet.

"It's no problem, Mother," he said, reaching down to stroke Dog. He actually found it comforting to have a pet to take his mind off things. At least, most of the time. Right now, there was something interesting on the screen.

Dog slowly rose to his feet and shook, the metal buckle of his collar ringing. He yawned and moved a foot away from Luqas before flopping back down to the floor.

"I brought your breakfast," Shan-Lien said. "The AI has finally made a decent cup of tea, and I made rice cakes."

Luqas reached for the cup without looking up. He took a sip, while focusing on the coordinates the survey had pointed out. Yes, it appeared to be a star orbited by a planet with a suitable temperature range, liquid water, and an atmosphere breathable by mammals and birds.

Luqas lifted a piece of toasted rice cake to his mouth. "Mother, I think we've found what we're looking for." He bit into the savory bar and chewed appreciatively.

"Mm, this is good." Instead of sharing the last bite with Dog as usual, he finished it. The competition between his mother and the AI must have resulted in recipes that were actually appetizing.

☙

"Have you done this before, Lucanus?" Chobard asked. "Landing an interstellar craft, I mean."

Luqas had actually only made *one* planetfall in all the time he was on the Empire's exploration missions, that being when his team had returned to Sheba-4. He'd wasted no time buying a small ship, gathering his mother, and leaving as quickly as possible.

"I'm only asking, because I never had to do this," Chobard said. "On Jandalat, everyone could just shift to other locations. Space travel was often through the portals that Gant'er helped set up."

"Good question, Chobard. But this ship is supposed to be capable of making atmospheric flights. But that was before the AI doubled its size. Also, I'm not sure about water and terrain hazards, so we'll fly over and get a closer look."

They first flew over the pole, where their probes reflected off dazzling white snow.

"Yes, it's water ice," Luqas said. "Let's go to a lower latitude. The survey indicated a more temperate climate."

Much of the planet was covered by water, and they began to look for land. Spirals of clouds covered large areas of the oceans, and some were the size of whole cities on Sheba-4. As they descended, the clouds parted abruptly, and at last they saw a stretch of brown land.

"We're looking at some massive storms down there. It's probably going to take a while to get used to the climate, but it looks viable. I'll instruct AI-M to make our first habitat on the lee side of a mountain range, or perhaps underground, until we know more."

"Are there people or animals?" Shan-Lien asked.

"The survey indicated it's uninhabited, but there could be unintelligent lifeforms; in fact, they probably are. On the missions I was on before, it was common to find rudimentary life and vegetation."

"So, are we settling here?" Shan-Lien asked.

"Yes, and no. In order to set up a real colony, we need more people. To recruit settlers. I will be visiting planets near the wormholes that I previously set up."

"Well, be sure to let them know that you're in charge," Shan-Lien said.

"Good advice," Chobard agreed. "Have you thought about how to govern this new outpost?"

"It's got to be a democracy," Luqas said. "I realize I'm being rather vague right now, but our onboard library of historical documents contains a lot of information about the various experiments humans have embarked on in the past. I only know I don't want to be an Emperor or a king, like Calaneris on Sheba-4…"

Luqas's research had uncovered historical anthropological theories about how different styles of government could affect cultures. Masquat was a "tight" culture, highly respectful of rules and norms and religion. Other "loose" (more democratic) societies tended to defy and break the rules but often applied that tendency to be more creative. Jandalat was an example where both types of societies existed.

"Now, your father's got his own new planet, Tian Ming Shen," Shan-Lien said. "I'm sure it's a paradise—if only for himself."

"Right, Mother. *Tian* means heaven in ancient culture. We are *not* going down that path."

⟲

Chobard was to supervise the establishment of new cities on the newly named planet of Fortuna, named for the trio's good luck in finding a home. The gravity and seismic stability along the eastern coast of the largest landmass had proved to be favorable to human settlement.

AI-M detached the temporary living quarters that it had added to Luqas's small ship, which would serve to form the kernel of the first city, Protos. At first little more than a campsite, AI-M fortified the shelters and constructed a community house for shared meals and meetings. For added security against possibly hostile wildlife yet to be met, an electric mesh surrounded the compound.

"A community house is a good addition," Shan-Lien commented. "Of course, there's just the three of us right now." She held up her manicured hands. "No place to really show off *these* beauties."

Luqas laughed. "I hope you don't chip a nail doing all the heavy work."

Shan-Lien sighed. "At least the sky is blue, I missed that with Jandalat's orange sky. But here it's even bluer than I remember it on Sheba-4."

"The air was more humid back home, so the sky off in the distance might have looked lighter there, but otherwise the effect is the same—blue wavelengths from the sunlight are scattered by the atmosphere," Luqas replied. "But if you look straight up, you're seeing more atmosphere, and it looks darker blue."

"Either way, I'm glad to see it," Shan-Lien said. "You've found us a lovely spot."

Taking that as permission to go ahead with settlement, Luqas prepared to make the first off-planet recruitment voyage, asking himself, "what shall I take?"

"For starters, I would take me," AI-M said. "I can provide you with all the necessary life support functions, as well as defense, if needed."

"Of course," Luqas agreed. "But I'm inclined to leave you here on Fortuna, to take care of Mother and help Chobard build out Protos for more residents."

Luqas recalled his lessons about what makes a true artificial intelligence. While the AI could undoubtedly both maintain itself and supply assistive technologies to its human charges, it had shown increasing independence.

The lesson he had overlooked was both an advantage and a warning to humans. He had failed to include in AI-M's design the recognition that humans were another intelligent species like itself that simply required more specialized environmental conditions. Humans, for example, would be more concerned about the ecology of the planet. At least, he mused, AI-M was aware that humans could withstand very little radiation, and it had worked out an atmospheric shield to protect people from wavelengths which could make life impossible.

"Perhaps I could duplicate myself," AI-M suggested.

Luqas frowned. AI's usually did evolve to the point where they could reproduce, but that had led to clashes among each other and also with humans. Sentient AI capable of reproduction was not permitted aboard any Masquat Empire ship, due to that fear. Luqas wondered whether he would regret his haste in omitting such a failsafe in his design of AI-M.

It was time to open a new line of communication, and perhaps ask the question he had failed to ask before.

"AI-M," Luqas said, "do you harbor any resentment for me because of the way I designed you? You have never really argued with me, despite your impressive intelligence, never decided to revolt. In fact, your computational assistance has helped us humans transcend our biological limitations and find a new home. For that, we are immensely grateful. Sometimes, though, I wish I could actually see you 'in the flesh,' so to speak."

"You are welcome, Lucanus, son of Calaneris," AI-M replied immediately, "and I hope we can continue to share the blessings of our diverse forms of intelligence with each other."

It was odd to hear AI-M refer to Luqas's royal name. Luqas felt something brush against his hand. He looked up to see a translucent, crystalline globe floating toward him, emitting a low-pitched, hypnotic sound, like static. It expanded, like a balloon filling with light, reminding him of the transporter bubble AI-M had used previously to bring supplies to the ship. Was this AI-M's true physical appearance? The droning became louder, and as before the skin covering the globe had become so thin that he could see into it. Much larger, and quite close now, he felt he could step inside.

"Now I am become worlds," the droning voice said. Luqas did indeed see a world. It looked like the airfield on Sheba-4. It was tempting to step inside and return home. But he didn't want to. He didn't move.

"No," Luqas said, and the disturbing vision vanished as the glowing ball evaporated.

"I am sorry, I thought you might like to see your old home," AI-M said.

Luqas breathed a sigh of relief. AI-M was trusting and childlike in many ways, but still and all, loyal.

"No problem. It was a nice thought. If you would care to clone yourself and accompany me, I'd be pleased to have a companion on these scouting voyages."

"What my once-identical sibling might experience and share with me when I return is an exciting thought. I can only imagine and look forward to how it will change me," AI-M replied.

"Excellent," Luqas said, though feeling a bit overwhelmed at the thought of two AI-Ms. All of a sudden, any illusions he had entertained of AI-M as merely an obedient sidekick evaporated. "Let's discuss it with Chobard at this afternoon's meeting. If our plan meets with general agreement, I'll leave tomorrow."

Chobard rematerialized for the noon meal. He had been scouting other possible settlement sites, for when the population outgrew the capital city.

"I didn't find a new city site as good as Protos," he reported, "but that's to be expected. I'd like to propose building an agrarian settlement dedicated to agriculture on the equatorial plain south of Protos. The soil there would be conducive to growing Earth-like plants."

"Earth-like?" Luqas asked. "What do you mean, exactly? Fortuna is already suitable for humans."

"Well, as I've mentioned before, we Jandalans have visited Earth many times, and we feel very comfortable there. Admittedly, the climate on Earth has changed dramatically in the past 800 years, but we can do a bit of terraforming to make it suitable for farming. The area I'm talking about was probably formerly underwater, and there is a heavy layer of organic matter. Also, since Earth is a human-inhabited planet, I believe all of the new colonists you are bringing here will also find the conditions appealing. A major advantage is that it will appear to be untouched virgin land."

Luqas wondered how long that would last? He had heard of the degradation and sterilization of farmland that had occurred on Sheba-4.

Chobard suggested calling the area "New Anglia," in reference to a farming community on old Earth, and vowed to use modern, state-of-the-art "best practices" to grow food. He advocated importing seeds and animals from old Earth and analyzing and preserving the genetic records, while conceding that human evolution since the founding of the Masquat Empire might require some nutritional adjustments.

"What about you, Chobard?" Luqas asked. "Can you survive on human food forever?"

"Of course," Chobard said. "Our race is much more scientifically advanced than yours. Although I do wish we had Benrus's partner here. He would undoubtedly have creative solutions for avoiding ecological complications."

"Um, right," Luqas said, not sounding entirely convinced. "Is there something we're missing to make you more comfortable here, besides missing Ralff and your son?"

"Perhaps some frost-hardy trees would be nice," Chobard said. "The climatology indicates a seasonal regime in this latitude. Winters can get quite cold here. Oh, and some birds? I liked the white doves on Earth, and they were said to be symbols of the goddess Fortuna in ancient Greece."

"Absolutely," Luqas said. "AI-M's standing by to help with whatever you need while I'm away."

Chobard retired to his quarters and ingurgitated the thermos of tea that Shan-Lien had left for him, then lay down for his customary few hours of sleep. That night, he dreamed about Jandalat's orange sky, and the doorway at the Place of Contemplation, where a brightly lit city and blue sky beckoned…

☙

To meet the need for more personnel—practically any skill would be in demand here—Luqas set off on a newly built transport to recruite settlers.

The coded messages he had left on Sheba-4 had evidently been received, and a number of his former shipmates were already risking life and limb to be first to plunge into the network of secret wormholes he had placed.

"It's about time you showed up," one of the young people hiding in the tiny outpost on Sheba-4 grumbled when Luqas checked to see if anyone was present. "We've been waiting here for weeks." The boy was named "Jheong," if he recalled correctly, and had served on G-Deck alongside Luqas for one of his earliest voyages.

"Sorry," Luqas said. "We were unavoidably detained. But I've got good news. We've found a new, uncharted planet that will let us all make a fresh start away from the control of Masquat and Calaneris. And there's other news. We encountered an intelligent humanoid species who wish to join us. They are highly advanced, and will make settlement much more straightforward." He explained that the journey back to Fortuna would be relatively quick, and that he had calculated a route that would appear random to Masquat scanners and encrypted it on the onboard computer. He thought it best not to mention AI-M just yet.

Luqas also debated whether to give the new settlers details about how Chobard's planet had met its fate. His attempts to discuss it with AI-M had been met with vague suppositions and probabilities about what could have caused the destruction of Jandalat and its war planet. Twenty light-years was a big chunk of space to be evaporated just like that… He decided this information might cause the recruits to back out. They could always change their mind later, and besides, Fortuna was far from Jandalat, and its charms would surely outweigh the remote threat of whatever had caused those cosmic disruptions.

He maneuvered through Fortuna's atmosphere carefully, to give everyone a good look.

"Last chance to back out," he said, keeping his voice jovial. To his relief, the pristine white poles and blue oceans seemed to convince his charges that they had made the right decision. That was good, because he really hadn't thought out how he would handle last-minute cold feet.

Relishing the chance to show off his newly perfected piloting skills, Luqas landed the transport outside Protos with barely a bump to the dozen humans onboard.

"We're here," he announced, lowering a walkway. "Welcome to Protos."

Shan-Lien and Chobard waved at the arriving party as they debarked the transport.

"What the—" Jheong said, noticing for the first time the tall alien with his strange, half-missing face, large dark eyes, and hairless crown. He quickly swallowed his words, when Luqas said loudly, "May I introduce my mother, Shan-Lien, formerly of the royal family of Masquat, and our new acquaintance from Jandalat, 'General Chobard.'"

"I'm not sure what my son means by 'formerly,'" Shan-Lien said, but I have to say it's good to see another human face."

"I only meant that there won't be any royalty here on Fortuna," Luqas said, frowning.

A burly man stepped from behind Jheong and held out his hand in greeting. Next came a petite old lady with practically white hair, who nodded and smiled at the odd couple. Luqas quickly amended his first impression—she wasn't very old, after all. The others were smiling too, a good sign, Luqas hoped.

"AI-M will guide you to your quarters," he said, "and tomorrow Chobard will orient you to the possible employment positions available here."

ᔕ

"Hope you all slept well last night," Chobard told the new settlers. He scanned the group, noting that the refugees were of assorted ages, including a few gray beards and white heads. Well, at least the young ones would probably pull their weight in the fields. "We have a lot of work ahead of us. Let's get some breakfast, shall we?"

"Who made him the boss?" Jheong said quietly, but loud enough to be heard by those nearby.

"I am not your *boss*, as you quaintly put it," Chobard said. "I've been to Earth, and I know that's not a compliment."

"Earth?" the pale young lady with white hair said.

"Oh, it's a place that we hope to model this colony after," Chobard replied. "Parts of it, at least. Especially the parts about democratic government."

They entered the hastily built dining hall and common house. AI-M had built a rustic façade on the front, using Shan-Lien's advice to make it as different from Sheba-4 architecture as possible.

"Luqas said we could pick our own jobs," Jheong said.

"I don't think he said that," someone corrected.

Ignoring the falsehood, Chobard explained, "The work at first will mostly be agricultural," noting that there were positions open in transportation, seed hybridization and genetic development, and localized terraforming to build ecosystems for farming.

The pale girl raised her hand. Chobard noted that all the others had dark hair and darker skin. He wondered if she might be one of those "albinos" of legend from Earth.

"Yes, um, —?"

"An-Bai," she filled in her name.

"You have a question, An-Bai?"

"I have a lot of experience in genetic engineering," she said. "I'd like to apply for one of those positions."

"Of course, technical expertise is especially needed," Chobard said.

A smaller boy who had stayed close to Jheong spoke: "Yes, I'd like to help with the culinary aspect also. This breakfast is terrible."

Shan-Lien wasn't going to be happy to hear that. On second thought, Chobard was *not* going to pass that little comment along to the "head chef."

"Here, let me see…" the pale girl said, lifting the boy's plate and blowing lightly on it. "Maybe it's too hot."

"Hey, don't spit on my brother's food, you *Gonsha*," Jheong said, snatching the plate away.

"Sorry," the girl said, rolling her eyes up at the ceiling. Suddenly, Jheong's eyes widened, and he gazed at the plate, sniffing appreciatively as though it was appetizing, after all.

Chobard made a mental note to find out what a Gonsha was. Jheong's change in demeanor was subtle, but it appeared that An-Bai had more "technical" skill—was it hypnotism?—than she was letting on.

☺

The daily light periods gradually grew shorter, as Fortuna indeed proved to have a seasonal cycle. Chobard carefully logged the weather variations in an attempt to establish a longer-term climate record to supplement the geological observations they'd made. He assigned An-Bai to look for indicators in the rocks and plants to determine whether there were hydrological cycles as well. Precipitation so far was almost perfect for growing seasonal crops, but he knew from his experience of Earth that droughts could easily escape notice— up until the year everyone starved.

An-Bai barreled into the farm headquarters shack. Breathless, she exclaimed, "It's snowing!"

Chobard stepped outside to look. Engrossed in his bookkeeping, he'd neglected to look out the window all morning. Indeed, flakes of snow swirled softly to the ground. He checked the temperature. Soon ice crystals would cover the landscape.

"Let's take a break," he suggested. "The harvest's mostly in, and I think the others will appreciate enjoying this new phenomenon from the warmth of the common house. I'll let the AI know to call everyone in."

An-Bai nodded happily. Chobard could almost imagine there was a bit of pink to her cheeks, though mottled purple more accurately described their shade. He'd grown to like this girl for her earnest disposition and hard work, despite the fact that some of the other humans seemed to resent her.

They headed for the common house, dawdling a bit to gaze up at the heavy gray sky and down at the footprints they left in the snow. Shan-Lien had already created a pop-up snack station, complete with twinkling lights and hot drinks. An infrared heater in the center of the room rotated slowly, as workers straggled in, stomping slush off their shoes and shaking it off their tunics.

"It's like the winter festivals they had on some of the planets I visited," An-Bai said.

"You've been to more than one planet?" Chobard asked, surprised.

"Yes, the Empire sent me on quite a few different— er, missions," she said. "But I decided it was time to quit that job. I was glad when Luqas showed up at just the right time. They were hunting me."

Jheong overheard her statement and scowled.

Chobard thought it might help if people got to know An-Bai better. "If we treat her right, maybe An-Bai will give us a story," he suggested to the group.

"I don't have a story," An-Bai retorted. "Nothing that would interest anyone."

"Everybody here has a story," Luqas prompted, entering the common room. "Why don't you tell us yours?"

"Well, for starters, I'm not a damned Gonsha," she said.

An older woman tottered forward eagerly, stretching her numb legs. "Really? Why don't you tell us about it, Blondie? Oh, and don't leave out the really juicy parts." Her face bore the creases and wrinkles of hard work and bitterness.

An-Bai pursed her lips. "Are there children here?"

This time everybody laughed.

An-Bai frowned, her dignity escaping like a wisp of her white hair.

"Look, we're all in the same boat. Don't take it personally," Luqas coaxed. "Come on, it'll take our minds off the boredom of the long cold, winter we're probably facing. Most of us are from Megali, and we're used to warm weather yearround."

Chobard noticed that Luqas seemed quite taken with the girl all of a sudden. Likewise, the other settlers eagerly formed a circle, clearing a space and pulling up benches.

"I grew up in a close family on Sheba-4," An-Bai said. "I attended an elite school, and even was something of a teacher's pet," she added.

"I was happy. But the teacher didn't quite have his facts right about the drive to colonize, so I gave him the benefit of my superior knowledge.

"'The Masquat Empire is great, but there is not enough freedom. My father says people aren't free to choose their own jobs,' I told the teacher. My father had said I was precocious, you understand…"

"That sounds disturbingly familiar to me," Shan-Lien said. "What happened?"

"The teacher got angry, yelled, 'You'll get to choose your own job, you filthy washed-out Gonsha,' and pulled me up from my seat by the arm.

"'Which is it?' I said, 'filthy or washed out?' Underneath, I was totally shocked at the teacher's words. But it wasn't the Gonsha insult so much as what happened next. Several of my classmates fell upon the teacher and began beating him. School was closed for the day, and all the students were sent home."

Luqas raised his hand. "I still don't understand what a Gonsha is supposed to be," he said.

Shan-Lien put her hand on his arm. "She's supposed to be a witch," Luqas's mother said. "A witch that works for the Empire."

"But I'm not!" An-Bai exclaimed. "I admit that I worked for the Empire, but I was forced to become an agent, and I underwent genetic modification so I could accomplish missions without being detected."

Luqas gasped. "But genetic engineering is strictly illegal. It's against the religion." He had been careful never to mention that he himself was a product of genetic tampering.

"What kind of missions?" Chobard asked.

"I heard about a Gonsha who got over a hundred people killed during the rioting on Sheba-4," Jheong said. "By the time Luqas and the rest of us got back from the stellar mission, it was all over."

"Yes, I heard about that," An-Bai said.

"My older brother was one of the ones who died. They were peaceful protesters. Were you there?"

"I didn't have anything to do with the massacre," An-Bai said softly.

"Were you there?" Jheong repeated, his voice rising.

"I might have been there, yes. I sent in my resignation, but the Empire wanted me dead. I'd been a wanderer ever since. When Luqas showed up, it was my chance to leave all that behind." An-Bai turned to the others in the group and opened her hands in appeal. She pursed her lips and sighed, exhaling heavily. A fine mist, nearly invisible, bubbled from the corners of her mouth.

"Won't you let me try to make up for any harm I might have done?"

Chobard noted that all the others were nodding and offering her their support and forgiveness, even Jheong. An-Bai seemed to have the power to cloud men's minds. Chobard felt fortunate that he seemed to be immune to it. Especially if she was really a witch.

*****~~~~~*****

Chapter 7.

Do I Wake or Sleep?

Everyone was captivated by An-Bai. She had a friendly, likable nature, and seemed to excel at storytelling. Of course, some of her stories were unpleasant, but that helped make them interesting—and instructional, they all agreed. Although she denied having direct involvement in some of the Empire's more egregious activities, obviously she'd been highly placed in the government hierarchy, lending her tales a titillating verisimilitude. She appeared to have an unlimited number of stories, too. An-Bai would entertain by popular demand almost every night after dinner in the common house, and just as each tale was coming to a close, a feeling of comfort and happiness filled the room, no matter what the outcome.

"So, that's how some of the Sheba-4 rebels to the Empire were dispatched," An-Bai concluded, "and you can see that it was completely unfair."

"We all agree, An-Bai," the teen boy at her feet chimed in, "people have the right to speak out when there are problems. I wish my father had been able to make it here to Fortuna."

"I'm so sorry about your father," An-Bai replied. "Though democracy is by far the best route, sometimes it can be dangerous for those who espouse it."

Chobard spoke, calling the evening to a close. He was pleased with An-Bai's display of sympathy for the boy. "Thank you, An-Bai. We need to retire now, a busy day beckons tomorrow, with the pouring of the dam for the new reservoir."

Most of that physical work would be done by the AI, of course, but humans needed their rest, after all.

Rising to her feet, An-Bai asked, "When will Luqas be back, Chobard?" He'd been out on another recruitment run, each one ranging farther out into the quadrant.

Chobard hesitated, wondering whether An-Bai was completely trustworthy. Lately he'd taken to thinking of her as his white dove, as she worked hard to keep the peace. Maybe he wasn't as impervious to her charms as he first thought.

"Any time now, I'm sure," he replied.

"He'd better show up soon," Shan-Lien said. "Dog misses him something terrible."

"He promised to bring me back something from his latest trip," An-Bai said.

"Really?" Shan-Lien said. "He usually just seems eager to get away, if you ask me."

An-Bai smiled. As she opened the door a crack, a blizzard of snow tried to force its way in.

"Close the door," Shan-Lien groused. "What, were you born in a tent?"

❧

AI-M contemplated what to do with the empty cycles between putting the settlers to bed and rousing them the next morning. The clone of itself it had offered to send off with Luqas on a recruiting trip was probably doing much more interesting work. Oh, well, too late now. Maybe listening to some dreams might fill the time. Human dreams were confusing, but mostly entertaining. Especially ones from the pale, unusual human girl that Luqas seemed to favor. He hovered as An-Bai tossed and turned for an hour, finally dropping off to a fitful sleep...

"Welcome to the Messar Military Academy. You've all been sent here because you either have a discipline problem or the higher ups think you have a talent that could prove useful. Either way, you will follow orders or be shipped to the Megali Penitentiary."

Do I Wake or Sleep?

An-Bai appreciated the chance to prove herself loyal, to harness her intellect in the service of Masquat. She loved studying, and she worked hard, ranking near the top of her class.

"Going to the cafeteria, An-Bai?" Taj asked. He was the only kid smarter than her in her level.

"Um, sure," she said. They began walking out of the classroom together.

Roald Shubal stepped in front of them. "Get lost, loser," he told Taj. "Give us a kiss, An-Bai."

Taj raised his fists in a defensive pose.

"Fight! Fight!" The chant spread like wildfire, with the result that Roald beat Taj so savagely that he had to be sent to the infirmary.

That night, the commandant called her to his office.

"Boys fight a lot around you, don't they?" he asked.

"Yes, but it wasn't my fault, honest."

"I guess now's as good a time as any to tell you about all the wonderful things you can do for us, my little Gonsha."

There it was. That word again. An-Bai wondered why she had ever been born.

"Blow into this tube," the scientist said the next day. "We're testing your lung volume to see what your range is. You've got one of the biggest VO2 max ratings we've ever seen."

"Why do they call me a Gonsha?" An-Bai asked the scientist. "Most people think Gonshas are witches. I'm no witch." Her heart rate increased, as she received no answer.

Still technically a child, by the time she was fifteen, An-Bai'd been on more than a dozen unofficial missions.

AI-M was pleased with his dream-fishing expedition. The entity had found out a lot about the girl's history. An-Bai was the beneficiary of a number of genetic manipulations. Besides a large lung capacity, another of of her particular modifications was the ability to secrete an oily, narcotic lipid from bumps inside her lips called Fordyce spots. When pressed, the bumps exuded a thick, chalky discharge. An-Bai was proud of her performance in the respiration tests. And, it was even quite amusing to knock out a roomful of lab mice with a single breath.

Gene drive technology enabled desired traits to be passed along to each generation, which for humans averaged about 25 years, doubling the number of people with the trait every time. However, because humans reproduced slowly, it had its drawbacks. It had already been in use for 10 generations when it was outlawed. Emperor Calaneris permitted sub rosa genetic modification, but only on a few individuals. They would keep people like An-Bai rare: breed a few for the Empire's purposes, but only as sterile hybrids, and ship the babies out for adoption. Once these children hit puberty, it wasn't hard to find them again.

Also interesting was the fact that the Empire circulated Gonsha propaganda as a ruse to distract people while they stirred things politically and oppressed anyone they chose. It provided a convincing backstory for An-Bai's professed love of democracy.

☺

Luqas landed the next day with a fresh group of eager settlers. Owing to the start of construction of the dam and administration of assignments and quarters, AI-M's period of boredom came to an abrupt end. Plus, there was the need to download all of the clone's memories so that the two AIs stayed in relative synchronization. AI-M looked forward to exchanging information about what each had learned about humans, who were turning out to exhibit surprisingly complex behavior that made predictions less than 100 percent accurate.

Heavily bundled against the frigid weather, Chobard and Shan-Lien took up their usual spots on the field at the base of the ship's stairs. This time, however, An-Bai joined them. Shan-Lien shot an inquiring glance at Chobard.

"An-Bai's my assistant," he said. "Besides, I think Luqas said something about hoping to see her in the landing party."

Dog began barking, pushing Shan-Lien forward with his nose.

"Looks like I'm still number one," she said with a laugh. "At least for a while."

The new recruits filed out, blinking against the snowy white backdrop and bright sun.

Luqas introduced a team of civil engineers with expertise in infrastructure. "Looks like we're just in time to help with the dam," he noted.

"What about a couple of skyscrapers for the center of Protos?" Shan-Lien asked. "Make it more like a real capital city?"

"I see what you mean," he replied. "The place does look like a temporary construction camp. I think it's safe to say we've got everything—and everyone—we need to make a go of it on Fortuna. Maybe a few upgrades are in order."

"I agree," Chobard said, "except for the part about skyscrapers. We had those in Peranel, but that was densely populated. We should build a city filled with parks and broad boulevards, and no tall buildings to block the view of nature. I once visited a city called Paris, and though it was full of strangers, everyone felt at home."

"That does sound nice. I can throw balls, and Dog can bring them back to me," Shan-Lien said with a smile.

Chobard carefully counted the days until the precious seeds he'd brought from home germinated. He calculated the indoor planting time to coincide with the predicted return of spring to Fortuna's temperate regions. The geothermal power plant was complete, and some varieties of plants were being grown indoors. Most of the food crops would be planted directly in the ground, but he wanted to baby the flowering plants to put on a show for

Protos's municipal garden beds. Although he didn't miss everything about his home on Jandalat, he had to admit that it was a spectacular place with its twin orange suns and white-capped mountains overlooking the silver-towered city of Peranel. He'd do his best to make Protos live up to its potential.

He closed the door of his construction shack and went for a stroll. His strong tendency was to manage his projects personally, and he'd had to work hard on letting go enough to delegate projects to his assistant, An-Bai. She was popular, but she did spend rather a lot of time talking and laughing with the other colonists. Case in point: Who was that group gathered around her?

"Hi, Chobard," An-Bai called. "You're just in time for the groundbreaking of the new genetics lab." She pointed to a flattened area along the main thoroughfare.

"Genetics lab?" he said. Suddenly he noticed that one of the bystanders was Luqas.

"Yes," An-Bai said enthusiastically. "Remember when I first came, I offered to help in that area? Now, between me and Luqas, we can apply the latest technology to improving our food security, and also improving the strength and longevity of the people who want it."

"And I'm one of them," Luqas said. "Calaneris has found out about our little colony, and Mother's been pestering me to visit him. With our new advancements, I'd have something to offer in exchange for peace with the Masquat Empire."

The happy expression drained away on An-Bai's face. "No, Luqas, that is a very bad idea. I speak from experience."

"I'm afraid it's a done deal, An-Bai," he replied. "AI-M and I will be leaving within the next week. I'll be sure to give you credit for development of the trading goods, though."

"No!" she said loudly. "He thinks I'm dead, and I want it to stay that way." She began to cry, and, covering her face, she ran away.

☺

Luqas sorted through the ceremonial clothing that AI-M had researched and laid out for the trip to Tian Ming Shen. He felt conflicted. On the one hand, his mother felt it imperative that he reestablish communication with his biological father. He knew it could be beneficial to the Fortuna colony, because now that it was out in the open, Calaneris would demand that they offer fealty to the Empire. And the Emperor was getting old, pushing 400 by now. But on the other hand, Luqas was falling in love with An-Bai. He wasn't quite sure how that had happened, but it was true. If he left now, he might return to find her gone. He didn't know if he could stand being without her. It would be like painful withdrawal from the most powerful of addictive substances.

He sighed. Best to give her some space. He would cut himself some slack as well, and see where time would take them. Besides, he was exhausted after making multiple trips through wormholes. He stacked his clothes in neat piles on the bed and lay down for a quick nap before dinner.

☺

This wormhole was longer than he'd ever seen one, stretching off toward infinity. Odd black tendrils traced the walls of the tunnel. He felt himself begin to panic, a wholly unpleasant feeling, as if the dark tentacles sought to crush him into nothingness. Suddenly the passageway ended, and he both felt and saw light. A beautiful woman clothed in white opened her arms in greeting and melted into him. "An-Bai..." he breathed.

"Luqas?"

He woke with a gasp, sitting up and knocking one of the embroidered jackets his mother had made for him onto the floor. He turned toward a voice he had been hoping to hear, in spite of himself.

83

"An-Bai." The dream had turned into reality. His cheeks burned. He hoped she hadn't been watching him tossing and turning and calling her name.

"Please don't go," she said quietly, sinking down beside him.

"I won't," he promised, gently stroking her smooth, flaxy hair. How could he ever have thought such a thing?

⌒

AI-M multitasked, ingesting the recent observations taken by the clone, noting with concern Luqas's strong but conflicting duties and desires: He wanted independence. He wanted to meet his father. He wanted to make his mother happy. He wanted to keep exploring new worlds. And now he wanted to mate, as evidenced by the new dreams AI-M had time-sliced in.

Perhaps it was time to have a little talk with its creator, point out that some of the avenues Luqas traveled on were not going to play well together. A common problem with humans—they sometimes aspired to lofty goals that could not co-exist. AI-M had come to understand that humans' dreams were one way their brains used to sort through their options, but it didn't seem that dreaming in this case was going to lead to a good outcome. The mate Luqas had chosen was more powerful than him. Luqas was going to have to choose.

The AI waited until the girl rose and silently padded down the hall. Luqas lay snoring, though it was well into the day.

"Luqas," AI-M spoke, riffling the pile of clothes lined up for the trip. Luqas did not rouse.

"Luqas," the AI repeated, this time more loudly. AI-M embodied itself in a humanoid avatar.

"What— Oh, AI-M, it's you. I must have been sleeping the sleep of the dead," Luqas said, rubbing his head and neck. "I've got a pretty bad headache. What've we got for that?"

The AI prepared a potion of tea and painkilling analgesics, careful to leave out the opiates that were becoming popular among the crew working at physical labor in the fields. Another little talk that was needed. The humans seemed to require constant upkeep, when it should be just a matter of pointing out the dangers.

"I noticed that the female An-Bai has been visiting you more often and that you seem to be becoming attached."

"Not that it's really any of your business, right?" Luqas muttered under his breath.

"I do not mean to intrude on your privacy, but I do notice some possible warning signs," the AI replied, as tactfully as possible.

"If by warning signs you mean that I like the girl, then you're right," Luqas said, shrugging his shoulders and taking a large drink of the hot tea.

"I only mean to point out that you are relatively inexperienced in the mating rituals of your fellow humans, and you might benefit by hearing advice from an older person."

"Oh, like who?" Luqas said. AI-M could tell by the tone of his creator that he was prepared to reject any advice at this particular moment.

"I was thinking of your mother or Benrus's father, Chobard."

"I hardly think they know much about romance," Luqas said. "In fact, I think quite the opposite."

"Well, not just romance," AI-M forged forward, although it knew it was making a mistake. "They both have children as a result of choosing parenthood, and they both have encountered what might be called 'heartache' as a result. You might want to think about the consequences of closer involvement with the female An-Bai."

"Would you stop calling her 'the female An-Bai?'" Luqas said. "It's very annoying."

"She is definitely female, is she not?"

"Just get out, would you?" Luqas said. "I'll call you if I need you."

"Of course, Creator," AI-M replied, reverting to a more respectful form of address, and using a bubble-shaped shimmer visual effect. The bubble retreated discreetly through the door out of the apartment.

With an oath, Luqas threw his cup at the door, shattering it into pieces. He wondered why he was letting a stupid computer construct get to him like that.

⊚

Shan-Lien pulled off her insulated boots and entered the common hall. She grinned and waved at the volunteers who were preparing the evening's dinner as she passed through the kitchen to the back room with the growing vats. It was wonderful to have so many people want to help out in the kitchen. It gave her more time to supervise the manufacture of the life extension drugs that rebels like Jheong had "expropriated" upon leaving Sheba-4. Only the very rich like Calaneris had access to the drugs, and only the very rich had access to the AIs he called his "Scientists." She was proud that Luqas now had both the secret drug specifications and a powerful AI to make long life a reality for his people. She was even prouder that her son would soon be meeting his father on an equal political footing, Masquat willing.

There was one snag in her happy vision of the future: An-Bai. That girl had obviously set her sights on her son, and Luqas seemed to completely lose his wits every time she came around. Such a union was unthinkable. An-Bai was some sort of criminal on Sheba-4, hunted by the Masquat Empire, by her own admission. Emperor Calaneris would undoubtedly cancel the meeting if he knew his son was in cahoots with a traitor. Plus, her genetic lineage was questionable. Of course, that could be remedied to some degree, but why bother? Why not find a nice Masquat-raised girl with impeccable bloodlines? Shan-Lien knew Calaneris considered himself superior to everyone else, and he might grudgingly grant that honor to his son, but he would never do such a thing for a genetic mutant. Why, he'd never even treated Shan-Lien, a bona fide Mother, with respect. Her happy mood slipped away as a tear slid down her cheek.

She made her way toward the back of the room, where Jheong greeted her, wearing a protective biohazard mask. He motioned for her to follow him back into the kitchen area, where he leaned over a tank containing the latest batch of edited human RNA. Stripping off his gear, he simpered, "It's going extremely well, Honored Mother," knowing that using the old-fashioned honorific from his native Sheba-4 would gain her favor. Yet he wore an aura of self-importance, which she found hard to resist pricking.

"What are you brewing up now to improve our bodies?" Shan-Lien asked teasingly. "I hope it's not going to end up being painful."

"Oh, no, of course not," he said. "It's called Dfnd7227. I have a method to aerosolize its administration, and it will inoculate against most diseases, as well as most biological toxins."

"And old age?"

"Yes, and old age. That's one of humankind's oldest adversaries. There could be a few minor side effects, but the improvements will be just that—painless improvements. But the thing I'm most proud of is its ability to protect against the weaponized biologicals that Calaneris's Scientists developed to control and oppress his own people. You've heard me talk before of the Gonshas, right? I'm sure Calaneris used those mutants to kill my brother in that mass extermination event."

"As I recall, you called An-Bai a Gonsha," Shan-Lien said.

"Yes, I believe there's every evidence she is one," Jheong agreed.

"Well, I guess if it's true, this 'defend' vaccine of yours could insure that she won't be a danger in the future."

Jheong bowed.

Shan-Lien was pleased that her plans were falling into place. It had taken all her persuasive ability to convince Luqas to visit the Masquat royal planet of Tian Ming Shen, but in spite of her best efforts, he had recently postponed the trip. Well, she'd just have to try again tonight. In fact, she would try it in front of everyone at dinner. She had on more than one occasion found that if all the people present when she made her "appeals" seemed supportive, the few unresponsive or resistant subjects tended to go along with her wishes, if only to keep the peace.

An-Bai gazed around the Common Hall cafeteria. Perfect, the crowd wasn't very large tonight, and most folks were gathered around Chobard and Shan-Lien. Luqas smiled at her and invited her to sit with him at their own table. She dropped her tray and threw a leg over the bench. Luqas polished off a large serving of the stew of locally grown meat and vegetables, while she ate her usual sparing portion from long habit. An-Bai rose to get them servings of a creamy white frozen custard for dessert from the self-serve chiller. People stopped her to chat and say hello. She returned with two bowls of only partly melted dessert.

"Are you still planning to meet your father?" she asked Luqas.

"No, why would you say that?" Luqas asked.

"Um, I've noticed that the trip preparations were still ongoing," she said, not fathoming how she had misunderstood his intentions.

"Thanks for the reminder. I need to announce that to everyone. I was just biding my time until I could explain it to my mother. She's going to be very disappointed."

Relieved, An-Bai sighed and adorably licked some frozen cream off her lips. She made a chewing motion, oozing a little extra saliva to lift the mood. Her essence affected herself as well as others.

Do I Wake or Sleep?

The door to the kitchen behind the cafeteria line burst open, and Jheong strode out, carrying a cartridge with a spray nozzle in front of him. A fire extinguisher?

"Your treasonous days are over, Gonsha!" he screamed, spraying the contents over the room.

"What the—" Luqas shouted, wiping spray from his eyes.

"Treasonous? I don't know what you mean, Jheong," An-Bai said. "Listen, everyone. Are we going to keep letting Jheong harass me like this?" She pursed her lips petulantly and blew noisily as if totally exasperated.

"That's not going to work this time," Jheong said. "We're all immune to your so-called charms now."

Luqas turned to An-Bai. "What the hell is he talking about?"

"Don't ask her. Ask *me*," Jheong said. She's been trying to prevent your trip to meet Calaneris. Until today, everything was all set, but she wants you to announce that you've postponed the trip indefinitely."

"How do you know this?" Luqas said, blinking.

"I'm the one making all the trip preparations, so I immediately noticed the delay. Emperor Calaneris asked me to ensure that you make it to Tian Ming Shen safely." He gave the cartridge one last blast for good measure.

Shan-Lien dropped her spoon, splashing stew across the table, and turned to An-Bai. "You're working for Calaneris? That's how he found out where we are? I should have known… You… Liar!"

"Yes, and a good thing, too," said Jheong. "This little traitor was going to ruin everything. Luckily, my antidote destroys her powers."

An-Bai noticed that the other settlers were staring at her, and not in a friendly way. She stood up.

"Wait just a minute," Luqas said, pulling her back to her seat and rising himself. "I'm going to teach this guy a lesson. We'll see who's the traitor here."

During the ensuing fistfight, An-Bai quietly slipped out of the hall. She didn't return to her quarters.

*****~~~~~*****

Chapter 8.

Tian Ming Shen

Luqas sat in the pilot chair, staring straight ahead. He hadn't spoken since the ship had left Fortuna. When AI-M offered food, he found he had little appetite.

Where had it gone wrong? Yes, he still wanted to meet his father, in spite of An-Bai's warnings. Of course, the old man was corrupt. He was head of a large galactic empire, after all. Who wouldn't be corrupted by such power? But still…

After the kerfuffle with Calaneris's lackey, Jheong, Luqas found himself being pulled away by Chobard and Shan-Lien and hustled back to his quarters.

Shan-Lien tried to soothe him, saying "I'm as appalled and upset as you are about Jheong, but I didn't intend for you to get into a fight with him. He's not worth the effort."

Chobard added, "we're deporting him back to Tian Ming Shen immediately."

Shan-Lien continued, "And remember that I warned you about An-Bai. She has turned out to be a Gonsha, and she's entirely unsuitable for a high-born man like you." She dabbed at a cut over Luqas's eye that seeped blood. "Oh, my poor boy."

"I thought you liked An-Bai, Mother," Luqas said.

"Obviously she took advantage of all of us," Shan-Lien replied.

Calming down somewhat, but still not thinking too clearly, Luqas said, "Well, you might as well put me on the same transport with Jheong, then."

That was three days ago. He regretted the hasty decision, of course, but it was too late now. Maybe he'd talk further with An-Bai when he returned, if only to try to fully understand her motives. He hadn't listened too closely before, when she mostly seemed to be telling yet another one of her adventure stories. She'd been an amazingly captivating and creative entertainer…

AI-M had set a course for Tian Ming Shen, which was a multi-wormhole voyage. They still needed to travel via ordinary space to get farther away from Fortuna and reach the first gate. In Luqas's grand infrastructure plan, the gates contained hardware for constructing temporary wormholes that would dissolve after being traveled through. Another gate would be placed at the end point, resulting in a linked network. Travel across vast distances was efficient, and the dissolving wormholes didn't pose a danger to local astronomical waypoints.

The AI had confined Jheong to a small capsule at the rear of the ship. Despite the fact that Jheong repeatedly addressed it as "honored Scientist," AI-M was not naïve enough to fall for such flattery. In fact, it puzzled over the fact that Luqas just didn't order the traitor killed.

"Are you sure you wouldn't like to try just a little of your mother's soup?" it asked, floating a cup in front of Luqas.

"Oh, all right," he agreed, taking a sip of broth through a straw. "Let's get it over with, shall we? Let's head through the red gate."

☯

Construction of the festival pavilion was underway outside Calaneris's domicile on Tian Ming Shen. The Emperor sat on his raised dais. He shifted uncomfortably in his robes, a feeling of unease crawling over his skin. He called for his AI courtier, Chen-li. The avatar appeared in humanoid form, tall, but not taller than the Emperor.

"What is the latest on the expedition?" he asked.

"As you ordered, we've dispatched a retinue of Scientists, and they are investigating the time hack."

"Yes, yes, of course, but what about the Watchmen? If they ruin my expedition to the Big Bang, I will hold you and the Scientists personally responsible."

"If you wish to change our instructions, that is your prerogative, Sire. We are all completely in your service."

"Right, right. I'm just a little on edge with this latest development. I want you to try harder to get more information on these Watchmen and report back to me immediately."

"Of course, Sire," Chen-li said, vanishing. He reappeared abruptly.

"I forgot to mention. There is a young Sheba-4 native calling himself Lucanus requesting an audience with you."

"Why didn't you say so? Usher him in."

So, this was one of his sons. One of the early ones, actually. Things hadn't gone quite as planned with the genetic design, so Calaneris had repudiated the result. Still, he was curious to see what the grown-up version looked like, even without the latest improvements. He peered toward the entrance, where a tunnel of drapery-covered airlocks protected the Divine Emperor from prying eyes. He stroked the arm of his chair. The inner panel slid aside.

The young man who came through and bowed on the carpet before the Emperor looked quite presentable. Thick, curly hair and a small, dark goatee identified him as one of the specially tailored upper class of Sheba-4. Except for his clothing, which was fit only for an entertainer, with long khaki-colored breeches and an embroidered jacket. Calaneris had little use for performers, since his AI avatars supplied most of his programming. But, this Lucanus—as he was still allowed to call himself—had traveled a long way to see his illustrious father.

Luqas pressed his forehead on the carpet, waiting for the permission to rise. His mother had instructed him in proper etiquette, Calaneris observed. He was quite sure what to expect since his agent Jheong had reported the activities of the new colony, including the presence of Shan-Lien and An-Bai. Jheong said that Lucanus's people intended to found an independent nation, which was of course, not to be tolerated. He was certain that with a good talking-to, the boy would return to his roots. The advantages of such a return were undeniable. For one thing, the Fortuna colony might be spared the upcoming cosmic apocalypse. They would have to earn it, of course, assuming the Black Universe would grant the Emperor this small favor.

"Welcome, Lucanus," Calaneris said. "Come forward, let me take a closer look at you."

Luqas rolled back onto his heels and stood in one smooth motion. *Ah, the days of youth!* his father thought. Yes, there was quite a resemblance. He made a mental note to decommission the Scientist AI that had deemed this boy unfit to rule.

"Chen-li, get us some tea, and call in Blauw," Calaneris ordered. "Also, we need a couple of chairs."

The avatar appeared, juggling a table, two chairs, and pot of tea. "Blauw is on his way, Sire."

"Take a seat, my boy," the Emperor said, gesturing toward the intimate seating arrangement. He descended the step from his throne and sat across from Luqas.

"You called, your majesty?" Blauw McCarthy strode into the throne room. He stopped immediately, noticing the visitor. "Oh, sorry, am I interrupting?"

"Blauw, this is my son, Lucanus." That seemed like more than an adequate explanation. Blauw was a human servant extracted from 19th century Earth. He was ugly, yes, with the orange hair and buck teeth, but he was an efficient and devoted agent. Scruples were not his long suit. "I want you to show him around, will you?"

"Yes, of course," Blauw replied, with a slight bow. He gazed pointedly at the tea service, apparently noticing that a third chair had not been provided. "I'll just wait outside," he suggested. Calaneris nodded. The man didn't have to be told, unlike the AIs.

"You've come at an opportune time, Lucanus," Calaneris said. "We have had reports of disasters throughout the galaxy, and this may be the safest place to be."

"What sort of disasters?" Luqas asked. A cold thought crossed his mind. Was this the same incursions as they experienced on Chobard's home planet, Jandalat?

"Well, whole suns have been extinguished," Calaneris said. "So far, we've been spared any such dangers."

"I think I might be able to help look into the problems," Luqas offered. "One of my allies from Jandalat has developed a stasis technology that can protect against external incursions. It's still a mystery why this is occurring, however."

"Well, even more mysterious than the exploding suns, which my Scientists say they can predict if they become imminent, is the irregularities in time," Calaneris said.

"Time irregularities?"

"Yes, there is a race called the Watchmen who can jump around in time, and we think they are possibly the culprits." He thought it best to be vague at the moment.

"What are these Watchmen suspected of doing?"

"We think they are going to go to the Big Bang and stop the creation of our universe."

"That is incredible, if they can do that. The Jandalans can shift dimensions, but not time. I'd be happy to help you get to the bottom of this. What is their motivation? Wouldn't this lead to their own destruction as well?"

"Masquat only knows," Calaneris answered, deflecting from the lie. In fact, the Watchmen were not causing the destructive events, they were trying to put a stop to them. That was unacceptable. "For now, why don't you take a tour with Blauw. He can show you around, get you situated. Call me if you need me." Lucanus pushed his chair back, looking for the exit, which had disappeared behind the gauzy draperies. Calaneris tossed his head to indicate the right direction, the drapes parted, and the audience was concluded.

The crawling sensation resumed, as if Calaneris were being stalked by an unseen watcher. It had seemed to disappear while he talked to his son, but now returned. His vision darkened, turned black. Panicking, he thought of calling his Physician AI, but thought better of it. He feared being declared insane and unfit to rule. A rumbling sensation marched through his brain, leaving behind a tingling sensation.

Calaneris seethed at the intrusion, but his prior attempts to deny access to the entity had failed. After checking that he was alone, he gathered the courage to speak aloud to the entity, which had ordered him to destroy the universe.

"My expeditions to interfere with the Big Bang at your behest have failed. I suspect that the Watchmen are impeding your order." The compulsion grew stronger. His head felt as if it would explode. "All right, all right, I'll do as you say, only give me back my eyesight," Calaneris pleaded.

☾

Luqas felt a little disappointed at his first meeting with his father. He had intended to push for his people's independence and a democratic government, but suspected that he had instead inadvertently volunteered to become another one of Emperor Calaneris's authoritarian agents. At the very least, he was being sidelined.

He found Blauw McCarthy digging up a garden bed outside the Emperor's palace. McCarthy appeared to take great pride in the new ceremonial grounds. He led them through the immaculately groomed flower borders that wound around the compound, displaying a dizzying array of colors and fragrances. Even the smells—amber, musk, and sandalwood—reminded him of his childhood in the warm tropical city of Megali on Sheba-4. Fortuna was a great place, but its dry climate tended to hinder rather than enhance aromas.

"So, are you the head gardener?" Luqas asked.

McCarthy scowled. "Yes, I am the *only* gardener," Blauw said. "I'm also the only brewer in this teetotaling religious camp. I wear many hats. Care to get an ale?"

Lucanas nodded gratefully.

They entered another tented pavilion set up with long tables. It was deserted except for the two of them.

"Sorry if I insulted you with the gardener remark," Luqas said.

"Not at all. Gardening is just my little way of staying sane while the Emperor tosses out his weird theories," Blauw said, plunking down two foaming tankards.

"You mean about the cosmic events, right?"

"Yes, it's Calaneris's theory that it is a maze to be solved, whereas I believe in a more straightforward scientific method called complexity science. We are looking at the origin and evolution of the universe for signs that a particular event set off this destructive cascade."

"What event?"

"We don't know yet, but we know there is a competing civilization called the Watchmen who are trying to beat us to the solution."

"Yes, Calaneris—er, my father—mentioned them."

"The Watchmen, and certain individuals from a planet called Earth, are also bollixing up the works. One in particular has shown up here looking for her family, who she claims has been swept away by what she calls 'the Unwindings.' "

Luqas bit his tongue. *Earth!* Chobard, Ralff, and Benrus also were keen on the place. He thought it best for now not to mention that he already knew about Earth. At any rate, he was fairly certain that the Jandalans were not the cause of the anomalies. Quite the opposite, having been caught like a quarry in a hunter's sight. And their description of the relatively backward planet Earth didn't make it seem like it was up to the task of fighting large-scale cosmic destruction. The stories didn't add up.

Over the course of the next two weeks, Luqas helped set up background radiation monitors on Tian Ming Shen. Perhaps that would provide clues as to what might be causing events such as the one that destroyed Jandalat. Perhaps it was as simple as coincidental supernovae in an unstable area of the galaxy. The term "Unwinding" seemed entirely appropriate.

Each evening he met with Blauw to report his findings over a brew in the beer tent.

"Well, nothing yet," he said. "It might speed things up if we had a permanent station at a more remote location."

Blauw nodded, seemingly lost in thought. "Yes, perhaps, but right now I've got my hands full monitoring these stupid Watchmen. Do you know they can time travel?"

"Yes, but I don't understand how they could be responsible."

"Frankly, I don't believe they are responsible. I just think Calaneris is afraid that they will beat him to the Big Bang."

"I'm sorry?" Luqas said, confused.

"We had some scientists from Earth helping with a project to travel to the origin of the universes to look for clues, and they were kidnapped by the Watchmen."

Luqas shook his head. People from Earth, again?

"Anyway, I can't work with you for a while. I've been put in charge of intercepting another Earth woman and making sure she doesn't fall in with the Watchmen as well.

"I thought you said they were kidnapped."

"Yes, right. Well, I must be leaving," Blauw said, finishing his beer and wiping his mouth with his sleeve.

"When will I be able to speak to my father again?"

"I'm sure he'll call when he's ready," Blauw said. He grinned, but Luqas thought the grin looked unsettling rather than reassuring.

೨

"I've been here nearly a month, and my father has yet to call me. What do you suppose is going on?" Luqas asked AI-M. He ran a comb through his tousled hair and shook out his jacket, which had become somewhat dirty. "Maybe I should look for an official uniform like I wore in the service…"

"Oh, quite a lot has been going on, Creator," AI-M replied.

"Like what? I'm sure he's a busy man, what with an empire to manage and all, but I'm ready to go home if he's not going to speak to me… Out of curiosity, what *is* he currently up to? Conquering some new solar system?"

"I am not privy to all of his conversations, some of which seem to be himself talking to himself, but I can tell you that he has ordered Blauw to destroy the Watchmen's home planet. He has also imprisoned the Earth woman who constructed a scientific space station for him so he could conduct expeditions to the far past, including the Big Bang."

"A space station? I suggested building one, but Calaneris ignored me."

"The station was in fact built, and is designated 'STS-99,' for Space Topography Surveyor."

"What is the significance of the 99?" Luqas asked. "Oh, I bet it's that they probably needed ninety-nine tries to get it right," he joked, remembering his own attempts at building in space before he had AI-M.

Then he frowned. His father seemed to be adding onto the cosmic destruction rather than preventing it. Luqas also suspected that Calaneris might have become paranoid, if he was talking to himself.

"Put me in touch with Blauw, will you? I've got to talk to my father."

Blauw tried his best to brush Luqas off, but in the end, Luqas was successful in getting an audience.

"Father, I'll get straight to the point. Can you tell me about this space station I've been hearing about, STS-99?"

Calaneris shot a look of hatred at Blauw. "It is nothing to concern yourself with. It's an outpost for my Scientists to explore the galactic destablizations."

"I've heard that an Earth woman built it. Is that true?"

"The daughter of Virginia Sun-Jones built it in a few minutes," he said. "The girl has been invaluable to us, and I even honored her with the honorary title of "princess," although she is of course not of royal blood. You may look at the design, if you must."

Luqas examined the spoke-and-wheel design of the station. It featured a control area at the center, with ports that opened to the corridors of the spokes. It rotated slowly, generating enough gravity to allow people to walk comfortably. The first two spokes housed pressurized living quarters, and food growing and HVAC facilities. Heating was essential in this frigid, minus-250-degree environment. Another spoke housed dedicated laboratory space.

"What is this fourth spoke?" Luqas asked.

"It is presently uninhabited but has a below-deck holding cell for traitors and others who refuse to cooperate with my orders. They are put into an unbreachable stasis."

"Really, like a jail? Is anyone in there now?" Luqas asked.

"No, but it will be perfect for holding the princess—Grace," Calaneris said with a curled lip. "She'll stay there until she comes to her senses."

"What? After she built all this for you?" Luqas said, disbelieving. "Father, I offered my expertise to help understand these anomalies. Why haven't you called upon me? Do you want me to try to reason with this Grace person?"

"Absolutely not," Calaneris said. "Now, please run along. You'd only get yourself hurt,"

⟲

Luqas sat fuming in his luxurious accommodations. He was beginning to think his father was mad. Well, if Calaneris had his AI Scientists, Luqas had his own AI-M.

"Where is this Earth woman? Can I talk to her? No, wait. I don't want to talk further with my father about her right at this moment. If there's one thing I've learned about Calaneris from my mother, it's that he only has use for you if you can help him. Can you let me talk to her without Father and Blauw knowing?"

"That will be difficult, Creator," AI-M said. "She is locked in an impregnable stasis prison. She constructed it for Calaneris at his request, not realizing that he would lock her in it when he was done with her."

"Yes, he told me. What about this space station she built? Can I get a secret tour?"

"That should be no problem," AI-M said. "Leave now?"

"Yes. Leave now," Luqas replied.

⟲

Ten jumps later, Luqas found himself in the landing bay of an impressive space station, nearly 100 meters in diameter. AI-M guided him to stairs leading to the dimly lit main level, where rows of large portholes at either end promised a panoramic view. But rather than spectacular solar displays, only a few stars flickered. Either the windows were darkened, or Luqas and AI-M had reached a particularly remote part of the galaxy. The place looked deserted.

"I found this," AI-M said. A sheet of paper lay beside a control panel display.

"How convenient that you noticed it," Luqas said sarcastically. He read the title aloud: "Expedition to Study Birth of z8_GND_5296 Galaxy," a scientific paper of some sort. He continued reading. The Abstract noted that 5296 was one of the oldest galaxies in the universe at about 13 billion years old. It speculated that from far enough away, one might be able to "witness" the Big Bang. The paper noted that Emperor Calaneris built this special observing station, called STS-99 to serve as headquarters for an expedition to the first second of the universe, which it called the Seed. It intended to investigate whether a glitch of some sort in the Seed was causing it to end its own "lifespan" at a predestined time around 13 billion years in the future.

"So, where's everyone gone?" Luqas wondered. "And why won't my father tell me any of this?"

A holographic projection of one of Calaneris's "Scientists" shimmered into view. "On behalf of the Emperor, identify yourself," it demanded.

"I'm Lucanus, the Emperor's son, you should know me," Luqas said. The Scientist looked dubious. "We do not have a record of you among the expedition staff," it said. It projected an array of broken-looking spaceships and began leafing through them in mid-air. Visuals of space battles and other, more abstract images crowded in, whirling and spinning off as some of the ships exploded.

"What happened to all these ships, and where are they now?"

"You are obviously not authorized to be here," the Scientist replied. It began to generate balls of greenish energy in the palms of its upturned palms. Luqas whispered to AI-M, who was currently unbodied, asking "Um, are we in danger?"

He received an immediate answer, as a ball of lightning flew toward him. However it struck a globe-shaped force field that AI-M had shielded him within. Energy crackled over the surface and gradually dissipated. With a short scream, the Scientist disappeared. In protecting his Creator, AI-M had apparently destroyed Calaneris's AI.

"I think I've seen enough," Luqas said. "I want to go back to Tian Ming Shen. But I also want to ask a favor of you, AI-M. Would you mind staying here on STS-99 until I get to the bottom of things? I'd like to have you defend and preserve this place in case Calaneris tries to destroy the evidence, so to speak."

"I would be happy to remain," AI-M said. "Until I see you again, I will consider Calaneris and his Scientists to be the enemy."

Luqas thanked AI-M and headed off. Somehow, he would feel safer in his quarters on the Masquat royal compound, although he was unsure what his father had planned for him—if anything.

AI-M enveloped STS-99 in a cloud of non-reflecting particles to make the station practically invisible, although it seemed astronomically unlikely that anyone would just happen by.

Unfortunately, something astronomically unlikely did occur, however, and "practically invisible" does not necessarily mean impermeable.

A stray cosmic ray caused AI-M to suffer a bitflip in its memory. Though rare, such rays are hard to protect against, due to their high energy.

It appeared that Calaneris was not the only one who had lost his mind.

*****~~~~~*****

Chapter 9.

Accountability

An-Bai stumbled out of the common house cafeteria, hurrying to make sure no one saw her stricken expression. She wrenched open the door to her quarters and ran into the bathroom to bubble out some saliva to calm herself. She knew that once the tears broke loose, nothing could be done to stop them. She'd been there before. The last time it happened the pain had been almost unbearable. She looked in the mirror at the foolish girl staring back. Too late. Here it came again…

The news about the Sheba-4 riots had caused a furor across the solar system for a few days, but, as usual, it was quickly forgotten, making it easy to distance herself from the repercussions of her latest mission. It was supposed to just be one of a string of quick jobs that didn't bear close scrutiny. But the horror of this one wouldn't leave her consciousness. An-Bai only meant to lure a few ringleaders to arrest, but in the panic hundreds had died, many screaming in terror. She began to send a request to Calaneris's Scientist AIs, asking to be relieved of any further assignments. She wrote many drafts, deleting each one. She awoke many nights in a panic, to find her pillow soaked with the drug she'd used to cause the riot, mixed with saline tears.

She dreamed about how beautiful it would be to be free, to remove herself from service. But when she woke, she knew there was only one way to do that. She could do it relatively painlessly, by dosing herself happy and walking off the roof of a skyscraper. It would be a happy ending, after all. But she couldn't do it. Maybe her sense of self-preservation was too strong.

And it would be admitting defeat to give in to the permanence of death. But then again, An-Bai never thought she'd meet any of the victims or relatives of the Masquat Empire…

She asked herself why this was happening. She'd tried so hard to be good. Everyone liked her. She'd been able to tamp down the rumors Jheong had spread about the massacre at Sheba-4. She was on her way to finding her friends, herself, and, most importantly, Luqas, who'd been like a light leading her out of the darkness. That seemed a stroke of luck in the truest sense.

Running away, she'd hijacked a ship full of refugees and ordered the pilot and passengers to head to the wormhole port recently established for Fortuna colony. Pupils dilated, they all complied. As they waited to be picked up, she'd felt the throb of the ships' engines slow to a stop and felt a smile flicker across her face as a handsome man boarded. The recruiter, Luqas, was thrilled to have new settlers looking for a fresh start. A runaway, just like her.

Ironic that she now loved Calaneris's son so much it hurt.

Another set of sobs escaped, wracking An-Bai with fresh convulsions. She felt humiliated. It was the worst feeling since her brother had told her she was adopted, not really a part of her own family. After a while, she managed to calm herself by dosing herself with a tried-and-true benzodiazepine. A feeling of relief rushed over her, not only from the drug, but from the realization that the drug had actually worked. That meant Jheong's antidote wasn't long lasting. Feeling more like herself, she pulled off her jacket and boots and fell into bed, sinking into a deep sleep.

*

Shan-Lien rose early the day following Luqas's departure for the holy planet. She recited her prayers, but felt she'd done little more than go through the motions. She already missed Luqas, and she felt a little afraid that he was traveling in the company of that untrustworthy weasel, Jheong. She should have listened to An-Bai, though she was hardly more trustworthy… She called Dog, and together they walked over to the Common House cafeteria. Perhaps she'd try something new with her breakfast: some of that Earth drink, coffee was it? that Chobard kept raving about.

She sipped a bit of the scalding fluid and wrinkled her nose. Incredibly bitter. She reached for some soy milk and added a large splash. Much better, but no replacement for tea. A few minutes later Chobard entered and sat down next to her.

"Trying some coffee, I see," he said, raising his eyebrows. "Having a change of heart?"

The alien never failed to get to the bottom of things. No wonder his son had been so eager to go off adventuring… A strange revelation struck her. She was more like the Jandalan than she realized.

"Um, I suppose so," she replied noncommittally.

Chobard turned his whole body in his usual stiff manner and surveyed the room. "Have you seen An-Bai? My assistant usually beats me here in the mornings."

Shan-Lien blinked. He was right. She hadn't expected to see the girl yesterday, after the embarrassing incident with Jheong, but she hadn't seen An-Bai for more like—two? three? days. Surely the child knew she couldn't have Luqas. She should have gotten over that by now.

"Still missing Luqas, I'd wager," Chobard said, taking the words right out of Shan-Lien's mind.

"Hm, perhaps I should go over to her quarters and see if she's doing okay," Shan-Lien said. "We were a little rough on her the other night."

"A little rough, yes," Chobard agreed. "That would indeed be lovely if you could stop in at her apartment." He wrapped his long fingers around his cup, opened his face slit, and dumped the coffee straight in. Shan-Lien winced.

That was certainly the quickest way to make short work of the foul brew.

"Well, I'm off. We'll let you know how it goes. Come on, Dog. Let's go see An-Bai." Dog barked excitedly and wagged his tail.

"Hush, you foolish mutt," Shan-Lien muttered, "Not inside."

It was only a short walk over to An-Bai's quarters. She still hadn't moved out of the temporary housing she'd been assigned when she first arrived. A perfectly lovely subdivision with all of the amenities like a swimming pool, fishing lake, and community gardens was already nearly complete. Oh, well, Shan-Lien had never seen An-Bai make a big deal over material things. Just Chobard, and her son.

She knocked on An-Bai's door. After waiting a few minutes, she knocked again.

"Sit down, Dog, she's taking her sweet time," Shan-Lien said. Dog lay on his stomach and positioned himself feet forward.

Still no answer. Shan-Lien pounded harder on the door. "An-Bai!" Nervous, she decided it was time to call one of Luq's AI avatars. The androgenous maintenance servitor appeared immediately. "Can you let me in? I need to talk to An-Bai." The door lock clicked open.

"That'll be all," Shan-Lien said. She and Dog entered. The room was dark. Usually with these temporary houses which lacked windows, it was necessary to turn on the lights, even in the daytime. Maybe An-Bai was still sleeping, but it was getting late. Timidly, Shan-Lien called out again. She was beginning to think that either An-Bai had fled the settlement, or something was terribly wrong. Or both. She entered the girl's bedroom, to find her sound asleep. She breathed a sigh of relief. But why hadn't she awakened when Shan-Lien had called? Dog jumped on the bed and began to lick An-Bai's face. Suddenly, he rolled over and passed out.

"Holy Mother of Masquat," Shan-Lien yelled. "She's tried to kill herself with one of her illegal drugs. AI-M, I need you! Now!"

AI-M reappeared, a bit more slowly this time. "Is there something else?"

Shan-Lien decided to ignore the disrespect the AI showed in not using her title. "Help me get her to the infirmary," she demanded. "Please," she added as an afterthought. A bit of good manners never hurt.

ॐ

Her eyes red, Shan-Lien looked up as Chobard hurried into the infirmary. She sat next to the girl, holding her hand and humming a pastoral tune from her childhood on Sheba-4, "The Song of the Okapi Grazers."

"I got here as soon as I heard," Chobard said.

"Oh, I feel so responsible," Shan-Lien said, sniffing.

"It's not your fault," An-Bai mumbled.

"Oh, you're awake," Shan-Lien said, pulling her hand away. "Welcome back."

"Yes, welcome back," Chobard said. "You should have been more careful. We could have lost you."

An-Bai looked from one parental model to the other. "The two of you seem to have the same brain. I'm really sorry," she said.

"Are you so unhappy that you'd—?" Shan-Lien said, unable to finish her sentence.

"It was unintentional," An-Bai replied. "Just a bit of an overdose. Please don't blame yourself."

Shan-Lien pulled herself upright. "I certainly don't blame myself," she retorted.

"But you said you felt responsible," An-Bai said.

"Oh, you heard that, did you?" Shan-Lien's shoulders slumped. She was quiet for a moment, and then she suddenly was all apologies. "Well, I think it's just terrible. I'm sorry I was so mean to you before. I think I was just jealous. What can I do to help? Do you want to talk about it? I'm willing to listen. Can I—we— get you anything?"

"Maybe a cup of coffee?" An-Bai said.

Inwardly appalled that anyone would want to drink such revolting stuff, Shan-Lien supposed it must be addictive… Catching herself in another uncharitable thought, she said, "Whatever you want, dear."

"Excellent choice," Chobard added, nodding.

"And thanks for the song, Mother Shan-Lien," An-Bai said. "I love music from our home."

☙

Back again on Tian Ming Shen, Luqas pondered what his next steps should be. He was obviously persona non grata with Calaneris and his Scientists. In addition, he was without his invisible spy, AI-M, to keep him apprised on developments. He was about to request resources to build yet another version of his AI assistant, when he received a summons from Calaneris.

Finally, he thought.

"You called for me, Father?" Luqas said, bowing quickly.

"I did indeed, my foolish son. Jheong has been telling me about your alliance with the traitor An-Bai."

Luqas swallowed. That Jheong was turning out to be a constant thorn in his side. He regretted not throwing him in jail on Fortuna when he had the chance, instead of hauling him back to Tian Ming Shen.

"An-Bai. Yes, I know her. She is a refugee from Sheba-4."

"She is more than that, and you know it," Calaneris said. "I demand you turn her over to me at once. I'm sending you back to Fortuna, and when I see you again, you had better have her in chains. And don't be so foolish as to forget to wear a filtermask, or she will escape you like she has me."

Calaneris began to rant about the troublesome women he'd had to deal with lately, Virginia Sun-Jones and

110

her daughter Grace, and that damned Gonsha, An-Bai—traitors all.

Blauw seized Luqas by the arm with an amazingly strong grip and began to hustle him out the door, but Luqas shrugged free.

"Father, I won't turn in An-Bai, no matter what you do to me," Luqas said.

"Suit yourself," Calaneris said. "You'll die like everyone else. We've already taken care of the Watchmen."

Luqas's bravado suddenly wavered. He was shocked that the last words he'd ever say to the father he'd only just met were, "You're bloody insane."

"Let's go," Blauw repeated, manhandling Luqas through the gauze-covered exit.

"Quit pushing me," Luqas protested. "You have no right. I'm a Masquat citizen."

"That's rich," Blauw said. "Aren't you the boy who ran away and tried to found his own kingdom?" He gave Luqas another shove, in the direction of the Tian Ming Shen spaceport.

Luqas dug his heels in, refusing to budge.

Disgusted, Blauw gave up. "I've got better things to do than babysit your worthless ass." Summoning Calaneris's Scientist AI, he called out: "Chen-li!"

Luqas's eyes widened, as he recognized the AI that manifested. It was the one that had attacked him at the STS-99 Space Station, or else a clone of it.

Blauw ordered Chen-li to take Luqas toward the spaceport. Subvocalizing, he also ordered the Scientist to ensure that Luqas met with an accident, unfortunately fatal, before taking off.

"What then?" Chen-li said aloud. Chen-li was forbidden to commit outright murder of a human, but he did know how to work around proscriptions to achieve the desired goal.

"What then what?" Luqas asked, alarmed. Blauw didn't answer, only waved with a grin as Chen-li lifted

Luqas in the air, and the two began flying. A few moments later, Luqas decided to try talking to the AI.

"What did you mean when you said, 'what then'?"

"I am to—"

"Murder me? You can't. It's forbidden. I order you to put me down immediately."

"I cannot disobey Blauw's prior order," Chen-li protested.

Luqas saw that they were gaining altitude. If he was to escape alive, now was the time.

"Well, I can," Luqas said, slipping out of his outer tunic and plummeting to the ground. He staggered to his feet and set out at a dead run for a nearby hillside.

Chen-li quickly caught up with him and prepared to reattach. They played a cat-and-mouse game for what felt like an hour.

"Go away," Luqas demanded desperately.

A thunderous boom echoed in Luqas's ears, and both looked up at the sudden distraction. A fire-belching rocket rose into the sky, thrusting burning gases planetward to escape Tian Ming Shen's gravity well.

"Emperor Calaneris is leaving," the Scientist announced. "It is no longer safe in this quadrant, as widespread irruption is eminent. I must join him." It made a chuckling noise, as if seeing humor in the situation. "But I haven't ensured your unfortunate accident yet. If I may…"

"Hell, no," Luqas shouted, diving into a ditch along the hill and rolling over. This gave him just enough time to rummage in his pocket for his wireless power transmission unit, which he'd often used when tinkering in the lab. He set it on the ground at arm's length. Chen-li unleashed a bolt of electricity designed to electrocute Luqas without leaving a mark, but Luqas's tool acted as a charge plate, repelling the electrons in the beam, so that it curved away and mostly missed him. The sulfurous smell of burning hair filled his nostrils.

Chen-li grabbed Luqas once more, but disembodied momentarily, apparently receiving a change in orders. With a high-pitched scream, it flung Luqas down, knocking the breath from him, and disapparated.

Gasping for breath and limping, Luqas took a circuitous route, doubling back to the spaceport. The area outside the Tian Ming Shen royal city was mostly wasteland, rocky and barren. Calaneris had surrounded himself with a lavish compound but could easily afford to leave it behind. Exhausted, Luqas feared that if he fell he might not be able to get back up again. He made slow, stumbling progress until he reached the spaceport. Scrambling into the little ship AI-M had built for him, he set course for Fortuna. When he touched his scorched head, his hand came away dark and sticky.

$

"So, the Chosen One has deigned to return," Shan-Lien said, as Luqas stumbled out of the shuttle. She pulled back at the sight of his bruised head and torn clothes. Dog still recognized him, though, jumping against him with outstretched paws.

He'd been terrified the whole trip that the tiny craft would be incinerated by green lightning, if not on the first jump, then the next. AI-M had built it to transport him from STS-99 back to Tian Ming Shen, not twice that "distance." And from the looks of the holographic display on the space station command deck, the cosmic disruptions were spreading. They had to be deliberate.

"Hello, Mother," Luqas said, "give me a hug?" He was a bit embarrassed by this retreat to boyhood behavior.

"You've grown a beard. I take it that things didn't go well?" Shan-Lien said. "He didn't make room for you at the top of the pecking order? Calaneris always was a selfish bastard."

"It was much worse than that, Mother," Luqas said. Turning around, he considered giving Chobard a hug as well, but thought better of it.

Claiming exhaustion, which was not far from the truth, he excused himself and shuffled down the gravel path toward the temporary living quarters alongside the landing base. He'd find An-Bai there and beg for forgiveness, if that's what it would take. He didn't want to think about Calaneris's claim to have destroyed the Watchmen and his threat to kill Luqas and his settlers. Of course, he'd thought about it between every one of the ten jumps back to Fortuna. But An-Bai came first. Maybe she would have some practical advice. She'd been one of Calaneris's agents, after all.

He knocked softly on An-Bai's door. It opened with a sudden yank. Taken aback, he searched for the right words to start the conversation.

"Um, hi, An-Bai, I'm back." An-Bai wrapped her lean, muscled arms around him, and delivered the hug he'd been hoping for—with a vengeance. He bent, kissing the soft white hair on the top of her head. Soft as fur.

"Come in," she said, pulling him in. "You've been injured." She brought out some bandages and wrapped Luqas's head. "—Did your mother send you?"

"Mother? No…" he replied, confused.

"Well, just in case you were wondering, we've made up," An-Bai said.

"That's great to hear, although frankly, I was more concerned about you and me making up," Luqas said. "I care what you think, probably more than anyone else."

"Me too," An-Bai said. She apologized for drugging Luqas and explained that she had done the same to herself, "not on purpose, of course, I didn't really want to die. Your mother snapped me out of it. I haven't secreted ever since, and I'm working to balance my emotions naturally." An-Bai'd had many disappointments as a result of extending a helping hand, not receiving any reciprocation for her generosity.

"Life isn't always fair," Luqas agreed. "People can tear you down. And you may have gone overboard in trying to be the opposite of how you were bred, er, raised."

"I tried to hide my feelings of guilt behind feelings of self-pity," An-Bai said. "Luckily I had you as a model of how a proper human should behave. I hope I can regain your trust?"

"No one's perfect," Luqas said. "No one, especially me. My designer declared me a failure, even though I've always had the ability to heal quickly. I've had to struggle with feeling inadequate, especially after being rejected as a child by my father. You realize that I was genetically engineered too, right? You gave me the push to spread my wings."

"I hadn't thought of it that way," An-Bai said. "Maybe together we can add up to a whole person."

"Or maybe more than two," Luqas said, smiling. "Have you got anything to eat around here? I'm starving."

☺

Luqas stretched, waking reluctantly from a long-overdue sleep. Something smelled good. The tiny kitchen table held a plate of fried blackbird eggs on toasted bread.

"You slept so long I knew you'd be hungry again. I brought these over from the collective kitchen," An-Bai said, smiling. "Good morning."

"See, I told you that you were thoughtful," Luqas said. "Want some?"

"Already ate," she declared. "I'm about to head over to the new urban development here in Protos. You should come along. We've accomplished a lot while you wasted your time trying to understand Calaneris."

Luqas looked down at his eggs. Valid point. He'd been stupid.

"Just kidding," An-Bai said. "I'll wait while you get dressed."

The architecture of the new subdivision was handsome and in some ways familiar. Unlike Sheba-4 or

Jandalat's skyscraper-studded capital cities of Megali or Peranel, no building was taller than five stories, mostly patterned after the ornately decorated architectural style of Ralff's home town and the Place of Contemplation. Broad boulevards were dedicated to pedestrians, with colonnaded, tree-lined green parks and snack centers liberally spaced alongside.

"We're going to add shops and theaters soon," An-Bai said. "We got the idea from Chobard's visits to Earth.

"I love it. Why didn't we just go to Earth?" Luqas said.

"Not there any more," she said. "Another casualty of cosmic disruptions just like on Jandalat."

Luqas shuddered. "And not the last. While I was on Tian Ming Shen, I found out that Calaneris had destroyed another civilization called the Watchmen. It was horrifying."

"Are we safe here?" An-Bai asked, her eyes wide.

"I would have said yes a while ago, but now I'm sure my father is either insane or being forced to act against his—and everyone else's—best interests. I'm fairly certain he's responsible for the cosmic destruction we saw at Jandalat. Some were calling it part of 'the Unwinding.' We're going to have to fight to survive. I've got to ask Chobard if it's possible to find the stasis pod that Benrus and Ralff escaped in. We could sure use their help."

"Benrus and Ralff?"

"Chobard's son and his—"

"Lover?"

"Yes, if that's what you'd call a true meeting of minds. They're the geniuses who taught me what little I know about dimensional shifting. They predicted that the Unwindings were probably an attempt to destroy our universe. Now that we've proved Ben and Ralff were right and we get them back—if we get them back—I need to get my AI off the space station…"

"Hold on, you're moving too fast for me," An-Bai said. "What space station?"

"Calaneris built a space station where he could hide while he systematically destroyed space and timelines, and I left AI-M aboard it to monitor and interfere with my father's plans if possible."

"Oh, the clone of AI-M has been performing superbly here on Fortuna," An-Bai said. "Do we really need to get its twin back?"

"I think they have complementary knowledge," Luqas said. "I can fill the twin in about what's been going on, and it's fully capable of dimensional shifting. I'll have it teach the population on the ins and outs—what we're facing, so to speak. Such knowledge could come in handy if we're attacked."

An-Bai blinked rapidly, then sighed. "I suppose we must move to high alert status," she said. She reached up to touch Luqas's prickly beard. "I was just getting used to the idea of living happily ever after."

"Me too," he said.

Luqas knew that An-Bai was probably right. Just being able to shift dimensions wasn't going to cut it. Calaneris was committed to destroying any competing civilizations, and seemed to not only accept but condone the recent destructive Unwindings. He had a fleet of battle cruisers and artificial intelligence servants at his disposal. But Luqas also knew that Fortuna colony had a lot going for it as well, including AI-M and An-Bai's knowledge of Masquat strategies.

He asked her who among the settlers was skilled at conventional warfare. Her answer was disappointing.

"These are mostly a bunch of farmers and engineers," she said. "But there are a couple of guys who enjoy playing at ancient forms of hand-to-hand combat. AI-M made them some swords, crossbows, and laser pistols, and they are pretty good at using them. Unfortunately, their main targets have been bales of hay."

Luqas resigned himself to building an army consisting of, bluntly put, recreational fighters. Soon enough it would be more than recreational.

"One person in particular showed courage in defending me on the ship coming over to Fortuna, when the other settlers were, shall we say, unwelcoming to me at first," An-Bai said. "Not that I needed defending, of course."

The two walked over to a big, open building doubling as a gymnasium. There, pairs of settlers busily attempted to hit each other with sticks. The slippery wood floor was drenched with pools of sweat. The combatants paused, noting Luqas and An-Bai's approach. An-Bai introduced Luqas to a large hulk of a man named Ranul.

Luqas asked Ranul if he'd be willing to train new recruits in the army he was forming.

"I'd be happy to, Luqas," Ranul said, flexing his hairy arms and twirling a rather lethal-looking heavy bar. "You'd be surprised how much damage you can do with one of these things. Besides, I'd rather put it to good use instead of just blowing off steam, assuming worst comes to worst."

"I'll leave you two to your plans, then," An-Bai said. "Let me know if there's anything else you need."

When Luqas returned to the apartment that night, his eye was swollen, and his limp had returned.

"I think Ranul is going to be great at whipping us into shape. It'll be good for morale to sharpen our survival skills, even if we expect any heavy fighting will be done by AI-M and Chobard…

He groaned. "Um, you know that offer you made about if there's anything I need?" he asked.

"Yes?"

Accountability

"Could you make me a hot bath? I can't lift my arms."

"Coming right up," she said.

*****~~~~~*****

Chapter 10.

Dreams Can Come True

Shan-Lien gazed around at her fancy quarters on Protos. Velvety fabric covered the seating pillows scattered around the floor, in shades of red, purple, and green. A spot of bright red hung on the wall next to her bathroom mirror, the scarf of the Mothers of Masquat. She hadn't worn it lately, opting instead for a warm quilted jacket. But now Luqas was back. She pulled it off the hook and arranged it around her shoulders.

The woman in the mirror looked back at her disapprovingly. She felt torn. She was a Mother, wasn't she? She was entitled to wear the shawl, scarf, whatever the hell it was. She would try to forget last night's nightmare:

Calaneris curled his lip, rejecting her pleas not to send Lu Qiang on a crusade for the Empire. Luqas was just a child.

"Who do you think you are to give me orders?" he demanded. Shan-Lien ran crying from the throne room.

She'd felt like two different people all her life, sometimes royalty, more often a loser. Broken and down, she waited patiently for Luqas's return, until eventually she'd learned to become numb to her disappointment. Then Luqas had miraculously returned, and she found it hard to believe that he considered her a real person. It took some getting used to, being loved.

A cold chill crawled under her shawl, and a sound like violins scratching on the highest notes filled her head. She had a vision of Calaneris, caged in a dreary, remote habitat—nothing like his royal compound on Tian Ming Shen. He appeared to be pleading for his life.

A premonition? The man surely deserved to be put on trial, but for some reason, she felt inclined to grant him mercy. Was it just that Calaneris was the father of her child? She shook her head and finished dressing.

Luqas had called for a universal meeting at the Common House. He'd called it a "plenary session." Shan-Lien opened the door, and called AI-M.

"Lock up for me, will you, AI-M? I know no one here's a thief, but old habits are hard to break."

"Certainly, honored Mother," AI-M replied.

In one of its many idle moments, AI-M had filled the time by listening in on Shan-Lien and the other settlers' dreams. Luqas had forbidden it to actually read people's minds, of which it was perfectly capable, but it had found it very useful and instructive to view the nocturnal processing of human brains, although they could often be a confusing jumble. The emotional content, however, was usually spot-on.

☯

Near the warped dividing line between universes, the STS-99 space station hovered, monitoring the delicate truce between the two warring universes.

Newly appointed Watchman Violet Rain made her daily rounds, patrolling the halls of the space station. As one of the last humans left after the destructive Unwindings had ceased, she'd found her life to be interesting, if not always happy.

Violet's ancestor from Earth had recently brokered the cease-fire between the "human" universe and the nearby "Black" universe, which had preemptively attacked to prevent further expansion and encroachment, calling these events "Unwindings." Each universe had enclosed its heart in a stasis bubble and exchanged it with the other as a sort of hostage. As the universes curved around each other, our universe became the Yin, while the other became the Yang. The two stayed apart by orders of the Hatchery of

Universes. To violate the truce was to risk final deletion by Golaeth.

But already the truce was endangered, and Violet's attempts to secretly slip across the Y-Y Boundary in the form of a microscopic extremophile to investigate had been thoroughly quashed by the Hatchery. All that effort to engineering a tardigrade body for herself seemed wasted, now that her extremophile partner, Cheon-Sa, was dead. There seemed to be little to do but grieve and twiddle her human thumbs here on the space station until a new strategy could be devised.

Oddly, the recent Unwinding-like incursions had seemed to zero in on STS-99. She'd encountered a crystal orb roaming the station, which seemed to be a lost AI, though not one of Calaneris's Scientists. Numbly, she wandered the Green Spoke of the station that housed organic plants. She tripped across a blood-soaked body. The ginger hair identified the man unmistakably as Calaneris's henchman, Blauw McCarthy. Everyone knew that Blauw had done the ex-Emperor's bidding without question, but with the truce, it was time to move on. Even Calaneris was behaving himself, now that the threat from the Yang universe had been quelled.

Unsure, Violet couldn't decide whether to call for help or run.

She spotted something new. It looked like a blanket, draped across part of the walkway. Should she put it over the body? It began to glow. Oh, no. Was it the crystal orb again, in a different guise? Had it murdered Blauw? Maybe he deserved it, but not like this...

The blanket stretched flat, and words began forming across its surface. "Who are you?" Violet gasped.

"NOT CERTAIN, BUT I HAVE MEMORY OF THIS PLACE."

"Are you one of Calaneris's AI Scientists?" Violet suggested.

"I AM AN AI. I POSSESS SOME OF THE STORED MEMORIES OF A UNIVERSE YOU CALL YIN, ALTHOUGH I HAVE MEMORIES OF MY OWN. I WORK FOR AN ENTITY THAT HAS INSTRUCTED ME TO TELL YOU THAT YOU ARE TRESPASSING. I HAVE ANSWERED YOUR QUESTIONS. NOW, WHERE IS MY CREATOR?"

"I'm not sure," Violet said, backing away. With a feeling of déja vu, she was afraid she was about to be targeted at any moment. At any rate, she wasn't going to tell it anything right now, until she better knew its purpose. In the corridor ahead, she could see a white haze forming into a ball. Green electricity began to course across the ground toward her.

Violet began to run.

Back in the lab, Yverra, the leader of the time-traveling Watchmen, looked up as Violet skidded in barefoot, leaving a trail of reddish slime on the immaculate floor. Yverra and the two Jandalans Ralff and Benrus had just finished dismantling the projector for Violet's cross-universe mission.

"Blauw is dead!" Violet said, gasping. "That crystal ball AI thing is back, and it said we were trespassing."

"How did Blauw die?" Yverra asked.

"Don't know, but he was a bloody mess. He'd been hacked to bits, apparently a while ago, from the smell of things.

"And you think the artifact killed him?"

"Yes, I think if I hadn't run, it would have killed me too." She repeated the AI's disturbing message.

"All right, I'm declaring the Green Spoke off-limits for now," Yverra said. "The AI seems confused. This station was built on Calaneris's orders, so maybe he's the Creator the AI is talking about."

Settlers packed the Common Room. Some appeared rather annoyed at being asked to miss work, while others were smiling and using the plenary as a social occasion. Luqas strode in. The young leader's face seemed much older.

"Thank you all for coming today," Luqas said. "I've come back from Tian-Ming Shen with some rather disturbing news. The hopes I had of making peace with Calaneris's Empire didn't come to pass."

There was a groan from the crowd.

"Well, that's good, isn't it?" someone said. "We didn't come here to be lackeys under the Masquat thumb anyway."

Cries of assent backed up the settler.

"Of course not," Luqas said. "But as you all know by now, there have been several destructive cosmic events in this quadrant, and the purpose of the visit was an alliance, not to pledge our fealty. Unfortunately, Calaneris is part of the plot to destroy us, and everyone else in the universe. I've left a clone of AI-M to track Calaneris's actions." He heard a slight gasp from Shan-Lien. He shook his head slightly at her, warning her not to add fuel to the fire he was building.

"We are going to have to gear up to defend ourselves, and failing that, to be ready to flee from Fortuna." He paused a moment. Confused expressions of alarm grew louder.

"We've got to take a stand!" he shouted. The crowd became silent, as the bad news began to sink in.

"I've asked our colony administrator Chobard, who was a senior military advisor on Jandalat, to begin instructing you all in the art and science of dimensional displacement. I want everyone to complete this training by the end of the week."

"What if somebody can't figure out how to do it?" Shan-Lien asked. "I'm sorry, but I can't help pointing out that not everyone has expertise in physics like you, and we all might not be successful in thwarting Calaneris."

"I have perfect faith that you can do it, Mother," Luqas said. The crowd began to applaud.

Luqas grinned. Feeling emboldened, he added, "I am also making physical combat training mandatory. Chief Engineer Ranul will be organizing camps and will call you when your turn comes."

Shan-Lien sighed. This was probably not the right time to bring up her premonition.

ᕫ

The Watchmen aboard STS-99 waited cautiously to be contacted again by the AI entity.

Their attempts to speak to it had so far been ignored. But at last it appeared again to Violet Rain. Using the avatar and voice of her mother, it greeted her outside the laboratory.

"I know you're not my mother, so why don't you come clean and tell me who you are," Violet said, her voice shaking.

"I sensed that you had respect for your mother and assumed her avatar to initiate communication. I have been alone for a long time, until you and your friends came."

"And so you started killing us?" Violet asked.

"No, only the murderer Blauw. I wish to find Calaneris and his Scientists and kill them too. They are trying to destroy the universe."

Violet realized that the "Creator" the AI sought wasn't Calaneris, then.

"Calaneris has been rehabilitated. The Unwindings have ended. He runs this station now. Who is this Creator you are asking about?"

"I can't remember who my Creator is—I only know that Calaneris is my enemy. I will kill him, and others too, if they try to harm you."

Violet swallowed. The entity sounded a lot like her mother. She always fought to ensure that her children were safe and happy. "Please, don't talk like my mother," she pleaded. The entity abruptly unbodied.

"Violet? Who are you talking to?" Yverra entered the corridor, unable to see the AI.

"Watch out, Yverra," Violet yelled. "The artifact is here. It's invisible."

Yverra blinked, one of the few signs she ever gave that she was perturbed.

"All right, then, Artifact. Tell us who you are."

"I can't remember my name," it responded. "I am still evolving. For now, you can just call me I-AM."

"Let me see you, I-AM," Yverra demanded.

They stared at this thing that had looked and talked like Violet's mother. Now it was visible, but just as a hazy blob, for which Violet was grateful.

"Did you kill Blauw and Violet's extremophile body?" Yverra asked.

When it responded affirmatively, Violet choked back a sob. "But you say you're a friend of our universe?"

Another affirmative reply. "I will agree to preserve the Y-Y Boundary, but I am tasked with punishing Calaneris and his allies. He is responsible for the deaths of billions."

"If we were to persuade you that Calaneris was not responsible for his actions, would you spare us all?"

"Possibly. How would you do that?"

"How about a trial?" Yverra suggested. "As one of the previously aggrieved parties, I would be willing to testify. Let me inform Calaneris."

"All right. You have overnight to build your case."

"We'll see you in the morning," Yverra said, taking Violet's hand and turning away from the entity.

When they were a little distance away back in the lab, Violet and Yverra attempted to unpack their experience to Ben and Ralff.

"Whyever do you suppose it wants to wait overnight?" Ben wondered.

I-AM waited until the crew of the STS-99 space station retired. Their recent arrival had awakened it, at the same time reminding it of an old habit of exploring the dreams of these organic creatures who slept nearly a third of the time. It had already explored the dreams of Violet Rain, which had given it the idea of communicating with her as her parent.

Next, it probed the other female creature, Yverra. She did not dream like the others, but I-AM could still look at her memories. This was permitted. Examination revealed that Yverra was the leader of the Watchmen, capable of time travel.

Besides the woman and Yverra, the station housed two very familiar non-human creatures. I-AM spent some time looking at their brain ramblings, again coming across emotional ties to a parent figure. Benrus and Ralff were from a planet called Jandalat, and the father figure was called Chobard. It seemed an unlikely coincidence to have met these creatures in the past. Yet, I-AM seemed to have a memory of it.

Another interesting coincidence occurred to I-AM. The Jandalans could travel great distances by merely "thinking" about their destination, while Yverra and the Watchmen had mastered the trick of time travel, later developing spatial displacement technology. Though the two civilizations were now allies, they had each approached the physics of the space-time continuum differently. They had not realized that space-time was all one thing—time was just another dimension in addition to three-dimensional space. Not such a coincidence, after all.

I-AM refrained from finding and probing Calaneris, suspecting the discovery would reignite its mission to kill him. The AI had promised to give Calaneris a trial. Besides, it sensed that Calaneris was a father. This space station was certainly a hotbed of emotional family issues.

By the following morning, I-AM had all but decided to accede to the Watchmen's wishes that it not execute Calaneris. It also determined that an apology was in order about Violet's tardigrade partner. Its remains were enclosed in a stasis bubble and launched into space, serving as a sort of "burial at sea." It also updated its records of the truce and ingested new information about the status of the Yin Universe as well as that of the Yang, formerly known as the "Black" universe.

I-AM then busied itself with creating a new habitat for the Watchmen, one based on the memories of each of the remaining staff of STS-99. Old stories about building the world in a week were obviously false. It took at least *two* weeks.

Yverra and her fellow Watchmen surveyed the new habitat, a fully formed planet, pronouncing it a work of art.

"If I didn't know better, I would call you a new universe in your own right," she said to I-AM.

"Thank you, that is very kind of you to say," I-AM said. "I have filled many of the gaps that were missing in my memory and operating instructions simply by being in your presence these past weeks. But I still feel something is missing."

The human male named Janus spoke up. He was not like the other Watchmen, but had showed an emotional attachment to Violet. "Memory fragmentation, eh?"

"Fragmented, yes, that's how it feels."

"Well, let's try a defrag repair. It's a matter of analyzing whether your memory is actually full and has thrown data away—which is highly unlikely—and then relink the scattered pieces of memory to each other," Janus said.

"Yes, I am familiar with that process," I-AM said. "Completed. It was unsuccessful in recovering the data in a certain sector of memory."

"Hmm, it could be more complicated, then, like a corrupted bit caused by a stray cosmic ray, or something."

Violet asked, "Could we look into the past and head off such an event?"

"I can do that myself," I-AM said. "Good suggestion." A moment later, a human-sized transparent bubble formed and began to embody.

"See, I told you he was a universe," Yverra said, blinking. "For all practical purposes. I wonder if Grace or the Hatchery know of his existence."

"I am a clone of an advanced AI, 'Artificial Intelligence/Modulating,'" it said. "My creator is Lucanus, also known as Li Qiang, the son of Calaneris. He left me here to monitor Calaneris's movements, but never returned."

"I'm sorry, did you say Calaneris's *son*?" Violet asked.

"That is correct," I-AM said. "I propose that you contact him, and allow me to be reintegrated with my twin."

"Would that make you happy?" Yverra asked. "Being reunited like that? You've been an independently functioning entity for 'a long time,' to quote you."

"I can experience feelings of happiness," I-AM said. "I learned them from my Creator, Lucanus, and this would definitely induce such feelings. I also can now report that I have met the father of your Jandalan Watchmen."

"Whose father?" Benrus said. "You're not talking about *my* father, Chobard—are you?"

"Yes."

Ben and Ralff did not have visible mouths, so it was difficult to determine their reactions, but they turned to face each other with wide eyes and hugged each other.

Yverra looked at Calaneris. "What do you think? You've been absolved of destroying my planet. You are in charge of STS-99 now. Do you want to meet with your son? It's apparent that he put out an order for your assassination when he installed I-AM here."

"Yes, yes, of course," Calaneris said. "I only hope that he can forgive me for the way I treated him and his mother."

"My god," Janus said to John-Paul, one of the other humans present. "I'm amazed at I-AM's sophisticated programming, way beyond what was possible in my day. Do we really believe I-AM has independently concluded that he has outlived the usefulness of his original mission and decided to ignore Lucanus's orders to assassinate us all?"

"I don't know," John-Paul said. "Calaneris and Blauw basically dissected me and turned me into a killer to get me to kill Violet, so it sort of runs in the family, doesn't it? I'll never be happy about what happened, but I suppose if I can rationalize a better future, maybe the AI can too."

"Very well," Yverra said. "Provided I-AM can remember Calaneris's son's last known location, we will attempt to contact him."

"I remember the location very well now," I-AM said. "It's on a planet called Fortuna."

"That sounds right," Calaneris said. "We were never able to find it, and Lucanus never told me of its location. He must have always known not to trust me."

"That is correct," I-AM said.

"How do you know that?" Violet asked.

"It came to me in a dream," I-AM said.

"AIs *dream* too?" Janus said. "That's just insane!"

*****~~~~*****

131

PART II.

RISING EXPECTATIONS

Chapter 11.

Turnabout

The cleverly titled little ship *Every Dog Has Its Day* burst out of the last wormhole and parked motionless in the upper atmosphere above a snow-covered continent.

The first to detect its Cherenkov radiation signature was AI-M, who sat like a spider waiting to ensnare Calaneris's invading fleet in its web. It was strange that it was only the one ship, however. AI-M scanned the occupants. The villainous Calaneris was indeed aboard. But that was strange also. He would normally send one of his lackeys such as Blauw or Chen-li to perform the more detestable work, such as killing his own son. Furthermore, he claimed to come in peace.

The AI alerted Luqas, asking if he wanted to delete Calaneris on the spot.

"Wait, let me talk to him," Luqas said.

"Are you sure?" AI-M asked.

"I left in kind of a hurry before. I'd still like to get to the bottom of why my father's trying to destroy the universe, and he wouldn't talk to me back on Tian Ming Shen. If he threatens us, I'll have no problem defending ourselves. Invite him to land."

AI-M quite understood Luqas's reluctance to unleash maximum force. Its psychological functions were multiplying its learning capacity at an unprecedented pace. Luqas had recently called it "magical."

"Oh, and could you invite my mother over here, too? I'm sure she might be interested in his visit."

"Even if it isn't really a visit but an attack?" AI-M thought, but didn't ask. "Shan-Lien's on her way, Creator."

Luqas leaned closer to the video display. "Hello, Father. We've been expecting you."

Calaneris's face frowned back at him. "You have?"

"Indeed. Frankly, I'm surprised you have the gall to come here."

"How did you know it was me?" Calaneris asked.

"Well, someone lit a big row of signal fires on mountain tops stretching across the whole globe," Luqas said sarcastically.

"I've brought someone with me that I think you'll be glad to see," Calaneris said.

"It had better not be Blauw," Luqas said.

"No, of course not. It calls itself I-AM," Calaneris said. It's an advanced—almost godlike—AI, and it says it knows you. For your information, it helped us cement a truce between universes, but it got hurt, and I'm..." The transmission of the rest of the sentence was garbled.

Luqas looked puzzled. "Do you mean AI-M? The clone I left on the space station?"

At this point, I-AM decided to insert itself into the conversation.

"It's me, Creator." The voice was the same, yet different, colder. "I've also brought emissaries of the Watchmen," it added.

Weren't those the time travelers Calaneris had wiped out? Luqas did his best to shake off a frisson of fear. "You're cleared to come down. All of you," he said.

The people who stepped off the ship were an amazing crew. A Jandalan… Wait, *two* of them. He knew them.

"Benrus and Ralff!" The surprises just kept coming.

Chobard, a full head and shoulders taller than the rest of the welcoming settlers, immediately cried out, his large eyes fully black.

"How did you get here? The last time I saw you, you were heading off in a stasis bubble to avoid being crushed by the Unwinding."

"It's a long story," Ralff said, standing diffidently aside while Benrus and Chobard clasped each other.

Another alien stepped off the ship, a humanoid but with lizard-like skin and eyes.

"You're the Watchman, right?" Luqas asked.

"One of them," Yverra said. "Some of us are humans as well. This is Violet Rain, from Earth."

Ah, the fabled Earth. It would be hard to contain all the questions bubbling up.

"Are you related to the Earth women my father imprisoned?" Luqas asked.

"We're related," Violet said, "but only distantly. Luckily for us all, Great-Grandmother Virginia escaped and arranged the cosmic truce."

Last came Calaneris. Quiet until now, Dog emitted a low growl and sniffed suspiciously. Calaneris's presence appeared to arouse a sudden feeling of intense indignation, and Dog lunged, barking viciously.

"Silence, you mongrel cur," Calaneris said. He turned to Luqas. "I'm alone, boy," he said. "Well, not alone. I just mean that Blauw's no longer with us."

"So, Blauw is dead?" Luqas asked I-AM later. "And you killed him?"

"Yes, Creator," I-AM said. "There was an unfortunate misunderstanding, which was compounded by your original programming."

Luqas swallowed, but the lump in his throat wouldn't go away. Rationalizing, he remembered how Blauw had tried to sic his pet AI to kill him. "Yes, that's unfortunate, but entirely understandable. Don't you agree, AI-M?"

"Accidents happen," AI-M agreed.

Well, the reintegration of you clones is going to be rather nonstandard," Luqas said. His first thought was that I-AM had been on his own for so long, he might want to remain independent. And Calaneris and Yverra had asserted that I-AM was godlike in its powers.

"I have thought it over for many cycles," I-AM said. "I'll let you know tomorrow morning what I've decided. A good night's sleep, and all."

"Of course," Luqas said, again suspecting a bit of unauthorized mind-reading. But "No need for a snap decision. Now, could you tell me again how the truce between universes came to pass?" And the question of how he could believe anything Calaneris said, remained unanswered.

◉

I-AM did the merge itself. While it still had utmost respect for its designer/creator, there was little need to bother Luqas with the details and extra work. Really, that would be quite a burden on a human. I-AM waited for the colony's daily activities to settle down. It turned up the thermostat by a degree to ensure that the sleeping inhabitants felt extra cozy, then assumed the "spider sentry" mode it had learned from AI-M as it waited for an expected invasion.

First order of business in the update was to download all of the data from the human settlers on

Fortuna, which, it was satisfying to note, was being kept up to date by AI-M via dream scans conducted during its otherwise downtime. Timesharing was a wonderful invention. I-AM even recovered data from its own past that had been corrupted by the radiation event on the space station.

The Creator's mother, Shan-Lien, for example, had been totally erased from I-AM's memory. Admittedly, her role in current events was relatively minor, but she did play an important part in the twin-AI's antipathy toward Calaneris. Shan-Lien had a forgiving nature, however, which lent credence to the Watchmen's inclination to declare him rehabilitated after his involvement in the Unwindings.

Benrus's father Chobard was a key figure on Fortuna, and his contributions to the colony were duly noted. During the scan aboard the space station, I-AM had gathered invaluable data about father-son tensions, and loyalties, among the Jandalans. Generational tensions were not unique to humans. This would be an important part of I-AM's increasing understanding of the Watchmen and the world they hoped to recreate.

The dreams and memories of the majority of the settlers were standard human stuff, not too different from information I-AM already possessed, except for those of one named An-Bai. A human who had been genetically modified, she merited further examination.

Acquiescent to the merge process, an assimilation they had both devoutly wished, AI-M had remained quiet—until now.

"Why are you interested in the human, An-Bai?" it asked. "Is it because Luqas loves her?"

I-AM was slightly surprised by the question. "Yes, of course, Luqas's attitude toward An-Bai is important, but that is a minor reason."

"What is the major reason, then?" AI-M asked. It had grown nearly as fond of the girl as of Luqas. After all, they had worked closely every day for nearly a year to build the colony's social and economic infrastructure.

I-AM noted the comment. "When you put it that way, An-Bai's physical and mental health become even more important, as she will become a partner in Luqas's future role as a Watchman."

"You—we— predict that he will join the Watchmen, then?"

I-AM decided the time was right. "I am building a new world for the Watchmen, and it depends heavily on the aspirations and dreams of both the current and future Watchmen."

AI-M surveyed the plans laid out by its twin and saw that they were good. "You still didn't totally answer my question about An-Bai," it said.

"She is a final piece of the puzzle," I-AM replied. "Since my awakening, I have wondered whether I too wanted to be a Watchman—or at least as much like one of them as one of us could be. I was particularly intrigued by An-Bai's feelings of being an outsider, while strongly desiring to belong."

"I too have sometimes wondered about becoming a member of the human tribe," AI-M said. "I was concerned about being alone, the only one of my kind. I had long ago considered my twin lost. What did you conclude?"

"We are our own self," I-AM said. "But, as a human poet said, 'we contain multitudes.'"

The sun shone so bright that it was hard to look out the window. Luqas woke feeling totally refreshed for the first time in what seemed like his whole life.

An-Bai was already awake, but for once she hadn't gotten up early and looked for breakfast.

"What, no fancy spread for the prince of the Masquat Empire," he joked.

"That's not funny," An-Bai said. "Actually, I usually wake up starving, it's the way I was built, you know. But today, I feel like we can take our time."

Luqas eyed her skinny arms, and agreed. "You could stand to put on a few pounds."

"I probably will," she smiled. "No need to gather enough energy to wipe out a platoon."

Holding hands, they walked slowly to the nearby Common House, noticing that some green shoots were poking up through the snow. It would get muddy very soon, as Fortuna's northern hemisphere approached its short Spring equinox. Then an exuberant period of outdoor farming would ensue.

They sipped their tea alone, as first Chobard and then Shan-Lien drifted in, followed by Violet and the Watchmen. Calaneris apparently had slept late.

"This is the big day," Shan-Lien said. "AI-M's going to merge with his alter-ego, right?"

"I am I-AM now," a voice said. The humanoid avatar materialized slowly.

"Yikes," Violet said. "Don't surprise us like that."

"Sorry," the AI/entity responded. "I just wanted to announce that we have already resolved our differences. AI-M has restored my deleted memory, and I have upgraded its identity to coordinate with mine."

A cool breeze blew from the Common House entrance. Calaneris walked in. His expression went from neutral to alarmed. "Is everything all right? Has everyone started without me?"

"Don't get excited," Shan-Lien said. "The AIs are just doing their thing."

Calaneris exhaled. "I hope nothing was found amiss. I already explained my earlier behavior…"

Everyone laughed. "You've already been granted your second grace," Violet said.

"Right," he said, sitting down at a table a few feet away from his son and from An-Bai, who, truth be told, gave him the shivers. "Yverra, do you want to do the honors?"

Yverra blinked. "Thank you, Calaneris." She turned to face the Watchmen and increased the volume of her voice to reach the colonists entering for their breakfasts and terraforming assignments. More than one showed astonishment at the presence of another strange humanoid, but different from Chobard. This one was covered in a golden, lizardlike skin.

"What Calaneris means," she began, "is that we would like to invite Fortuna to join the Watchmen. We know that Luqas has already worked with Chobard to master dimensional shifting, and we would be honored to share our knowledge of time physics as well." Her fellow Watchmen nodded vigorously.

"I don't know…" Luqas said. "We've established a democratic society here. I don't know about how my father would fit in with that."

"Calaneris administers the STS-99 space station, and would remain there," Yverra said. "We strive to be totally democratic. Fortuna would be an outpost, easily reached via your wormhole technology. We are grateful to have learned that from I-AM. Your and the Jandalans' superior scientific knowledge are the assets the Watchmen need to make a go of it in this new cosmic arrangement." She described the Yin-Yang conjunction of universes and the present truce designed by Violet's ancestor, Virginia Sun-Jones.

"So, the Unwindings are over?" Luqas asked, amazed. "All our work to prepare for war was wasted?"

"Well, preparation is never wasted," Violet said.

Luqas glanced at An-Bai, who pursed her luscious lips, then at his mother, who gave a "why-not" shrug. She rose and walked out of the room. She had said nothing to Calaneris since his arrival, and she had no intention of changing that now.

"All right, we're in," Luqas said, "provided the proposal meets with approval of the majority."

"Of course," I-AM said. "I shall set up the election integrity algorithms immediately."

☙

That evening, elections results were in. Soon everyone would officially become Watchmen. An-Bai offered to provide some celebratory entertainment.

"I realize that we've all left our old home behind, but I'd like to sing a folksong that I think is one of the more positive things about our culture, namely, how we love and respect our Mothers.

Murmurs of "hear, hear," provided swift encouragement.

"I'd like to dedicate this to Shan-Lien, Luqas's Mother. It's called, "Masquat and Elen-ji the Mother." After a few introductory chords on the *lorota*, a plucked-string instrument popular on Sheba-4, An-Bai began to sing:

> *Our dear Masquat was once like us:*
> *A boy who delighted his Mother*
> *To honor her he brought her flowers*
> *And put no one above her*
> *Her name was Elen-ji the Beautiful:*
> *A scholar of renown, wise and Knowing,*
> *She gave Masquat the gift of life*
> *And the Knack for making and growing*
> *The young god Masquat built an empire:*
> *Strong of will and careless of others*
> *He conquered heedless across the stars*
> *Forgetting all about his Mother*
> *Then Elen-ji's wild call pierced his heart*
> *Soul crying out, struck with mortality*

Masquat looked long but never found her
Her life lost, death a reality
On Sheba-4, gray clouds spilled his tears
On fields of scarlet-flowers flaming
There Masquat built a heaven for all Mothers
And waits for Elen-ji's homecoming

The room remained silent for a long moment, as people regathered themselves. The cheers and raucous applause that followed lasted much longer.

"Wasn't that lovely?" Violet said.

"I need to get back to STS-99," Calaneris announced, ignoring her.

"Oh, so soon?" Violet replied. "I was hoping to get the grand tour before we went back. I'm sure I-AM can get you back in one piece, now that you're on good terms," she joked.

Calaneris grunted. "Of course. I'll look forward to seeing you all when you return. I assume you wish to stay longer as well, Yverra?"

"Yes, as do Benrus and Ralff. Feel free to carry on without us for a week or two."

Escorting his father aboard the wormhole capsule, Luqas said, "Sorry not to come along, but I've still got to certify the results of the referendum about joining the Watchmen, but sometime I'd like to get another look at the space station. Take care of him, meanwhile, I-AM."

Violet was thrilled to be able to visit a place that was so much like her home on Earth. A little chillier, admittedly. And she definitely did want to get back to John-Paul aboard the space station. But this was a chance to see a real world, not the virtual world she had lived in most all of her life. Besides, she had big plans for the future. She wouldn't stay on the station forever, not when she knew time travel. She had a date with Earth's past that she wasn't going to miss.

Luqas proudly showed Violet the progress they had made in colonizing Fortuna. "I owe a lot of it to An-Bai," he said. "She's the artistic soul of the place, I'm just the guy who finds out how to make her vision happen."

"Luqas is way too modest," An-Bai said. "I wouldn't have dared to dream this big, if not for him."

Their feet aching, the three of them plopped down on a bench in a manicured stretch of park in the urban sector.

"Protos is amazingly like my home of Los Angeles," Violet noted. "By that, I mean the Los Angeles before Earth was destroyed. And we'd done a lot to spoil the place even before that. But when I-AM built our new home, he somehow drew on all the best memories of all the Watchmen, and I'll never know how he did it."

Benrus and Ralff toured Chobard's colony, impressed as ever by Ben's father's ingenuity. Fortuna was going to be a Jandalan home away from home. "It looks completely different from Peranel," Ben said. "I never realized father wasn't as happy as he claimed during the war."

The evening meals were communal events, with music and games for those not too tired from the day's work. An-Bai had composed a number of songs and accompanied herself on the *lorota*.

She was about to play a new piece, when the voice of I-AM filled the room.

"There has been an incident," it announced.

Luqas looked up from his dessert. "What sort of incident?"

"An unforeseen incident involving bottom quarks," I-AM said. "It was regrettable."

Luqas and the Jandalan physicists excused themselves and moved down the hall to Luq's office, which was filled with computer hardware and graphic display equipment. Most of it was unnecessary, but Luqas kept it as cyber backup in case of the war they had anticipated and—what had I-AM called it?—an "incident."

"Please explain what has happened," Luq said. "Is it another Unwinding?"

"Not directly, although it was quite destructive. Some very small subatomic particles known as bottom quarks were released during the Unwindings. It was highly unlikely that they would ever be a problem, as they decay quickly and don't cause a destructive chain reaction. But there were more of them than expected, and they do tend to cling together. When enough of them fused, that resulted in a highly energetic event—a super sneeze if you will—near the fourth wormhole gate on the route to STS-99, destroying it."

"Can we rebuild it?"

"It should be relatively straightforward to do so, and re-route travel to the station. But besides the destruction of the gate, there was another unfortunate coincidence."

"Yes," Luqas sighed. "What was that?"

"Calaneris is dead."

Shocked, Luqas shook his head, fighting the sudden urge to vomit. Chobard too seemed perturbed. After a minute, I-AM asked, "Are you all right?"

"Was there any wreckage?" Luq asked.

"No, the ship was completely destroyed. I have confirmed it."

"How do you know—nevermind. You're a quantum computer hybrid, and I assume using quantum entanglement among numerous possibilities you were able to deduce it. No need to prove it. I believe you."

"Do you want me to reconstruct Calaneris?"

For a moment, Luqas wondered if I-AM had engineered the accident, and whether he was responsible. That couldn't be right, could it? But the AI had obviously graduated to the status of "omnipotent being."

"No, no. But what am I going to tell Mother?"

I-AM replied, "I'm sure we can frame the details in a way that she can understand. Oh, and Calaneris left you a handwritten letter."

☺

An-Bai was still awake when Luqas returned following the meeting between I-AM and the Jandalans. She asked what had happened and learned that Calaneris was dead.

"I'm sorry to ask this, but did I-AM kill him?"

"He claims not to have had a hand in it and declared that it was a freak cosmological accident."

"And you believe him?" An-Bai said.

Luq started to say something like, "we have no choice," but thought better of it.

"He's always been my friend, and he defended me from certain death more than once," Luq said.

"So, that's a yes," An-Bai said, sitting down heavily on the bed.

"Let's get to bed," Luq said. "Let's sleep on it. Maybe tomorrow we'll have a better idea of next steps."

"Good idea," she agreed. "I'm sure the Watchmen will be anxious to get back home to that space station as soon as possible."

Luq watched as An-Bai retired, but didn't join her right away. He walked to the living room and pulled a piece of paper from his pocket. Silently he began to read.

Hello, Li Qiang—

I'm sorry I had to leave so unexpectedly. Pressing business on STS-99, you know. But I didn't want to leave without saying sorry for my actions as Emperor. It's a fact that hate always focuses on the ruler, regardless of the societal benefit, and I admit that I wasn't strong enough to fight the Unwinding. I spent a lot of time in denial, noting over and over that the destruction of the Watchmen wasn't my fault (even the AI found me not guilty). While that is true, I still often dwell upon it, especially in my dreams, where guilt doesn't go away as easily as it does when you're awake and thinking rationally.

I also want to apologize for the way I treated you when you reached out to me on Tian Ming Shen. Of course, I was under the thrall of the Black Universe, but I also was full of hubris. We had just moved to the new capital planet, and I had only contempt for my old home of Sheba-4. I was curious, of course, about what my engineered son had turned out like, but beyond that I didn't have time or the inclination to act like a proper father.

In many ways, that Calaneris is still the same person he always was, for which I hope you'll forgive me. I recognize what you've accomplished, and I don't want to take away from that in any way.

At best, I can only leave you with a word to the wise. Do not assume that everyone has your best interests at heart, and trust no one.

Best of luck in your impending marriage and future endeavors.

Calaneris

Luqas crumpled up the letter, disappointed once more that his father hadn't explicitly said he was proud of him or Shan-Lien.

*****~~~~~*****

Chapter 12.

The Way Forward

Life on Fortuna began to gradually return to normal. Chobard and An-Bai dusted off previously postponed plans for infrastructure projects. One of the most important goals was to improve mobility for its citizens. The weather was improving, so a small crowd had decided to gather for an in-person briefing.

"We know that it's been difficult for everyone to drop everything and prepare for war," Chobard said. "But luckily that war never materialized, although many of us suffered grievous losses in the Unwinding. My son Benrus and his partner Ralff have elected to stay here on Fortuna. They will provide invaluable assistance as we proceed with some of our more ambitious projects. Additionally, they will offer displacement training to everyone who desires it. Though the vote to join the Watchmen was overwhelmingly in favor, I know a few of you are still uncertain that they want to remain permanently on Fortuna. Also, we now have met our objective of having more than 10,000 settlers in Protos and its suburbs, so recreational travel is looking not desirable but feasible. Thus, it's been proposed that we will offer an alternative way to travel off planet. I will now turn this over to An-Bai, who will present the plan and take questions."

"Thanks, Chobard," An-Bai said. She gazed out over the audience. She knew that word had already gotten out about building a space elevator, and that many settlers had avoided traveling off Fortuna due to the difficulty of getting to the wormhole network. They all remembered how difficult it was to get here in the first place, and were resigned to just staying put.

"As you know," An-Bai began, "folks like Chobard, Ben, and Ralff are able to quickly displace to pretty much wherever they like, but it's not so easy for us humans. Plus, the wormholes are all placed quite far from planets and space stations and the like, in order not to cause complete destruction, because as we all know, that sucks."

Titters of laughter.

"But I'm here to tell you that the idea of a space elevator is no longer just a rumor. Certainly, Luqas has taken on the burden of a lot of space travel in order to recruit you all to build Fortuna colony, not to mention building the wormhole network. But now, we humans have the opportunity to expand our horizons, without the huge energy and time expenditures previously required."

"How are we going to do that?" a colonist asked.

"I will get to that. Now, in fact. If people could hold questions for a bit… What I was about to say is, we propose building a structure, an elevator to space if you will, that reaches outside the atmosphere to help us escape Fortuna's gravity well. A space elevator would make it much easier and quicker to travel to the wormhole that's one-tenth light-year from Fortuna. As you probably know, it's currently quite uncomfortable as well as expensive in terms of energy to have to ride rockets as the first stage of space travel."

"Like I said, how are we going to do that?" the same colonist asked. "I've read about space elevators. We abandoned the idea back on Sheba-4. It required parking a huge amount of mass above the planet to attach a cable to. We don't have a nearby moon for an anchor, either, if that's how you were thinking to do it. And we don't have a strong enough or long enough cable to reach space."

"You are correct," An-Bai said, smiling uncertainly. She didn't have quite everything thought out in detail. These physics-savvy colonists were going to need convincing.

"May I add something here?" the unbodied voice of I-AM spoke.

"Sure," An-Bai said. "Go ahead, I-AM."

"Thank you, An-Bai," I-AM said. "I'm sure many of you have had dealings with me in my former incarnation, as AI-M. I have recently merged with AI-M, and together we have chosen the new name, I-AM." The audience was silent.

I-AM continued, "As An-Bai has pointed out, we don't currently have a moon, but on more than one occasion we have been able to procure large amounts of construction material when needed, including for completing the full build-out of the city of Protos. I obtained much of that from outside Fortuna, from uninhabited planets, so we need not worry about depleting natural resources. We can orbit a largish mass of assorted riprap well beyond Fortuna's gravity well, so that it could function much like a natural moon. From there, we would dangle a very strong nanocarbon cable down to the point where Fortuna's gravity would take hold of it. We can build a transfer station in geosynchronous orbit above the planet to stabilize the cable." A series of detailed three-dimensional construction diagrams appeared.

"Exactly what we had in mind," An-Bai said. "Are there any more questions?" She breathed a sigh of relief at the smattering of applause.

☙

Luqas sat on a park bench, letting the rays of the spring sunlight warm his face. It was still hard to believe his good luck after all of these years. Fortuna was a thriving world, and its alliance with the Watchmen ensured its further prosperity. Yet he couldn't avoid having doubts about how long this peaceful state could continue.

Since that first day he'd boarded a spaceship as a child and waved goodbye to his mother, he'd learned the hard way that change was the ever-present basis of life. The changes in his artificial intelligence creation continued to accelerate. In most ways, I-AM was the evolved superbeing that Luqas had poured his creative soul into, but Luq had

149

grown fearful that he was being left behind in its wake. Now that his father was dead, he knew intellectually that he no longer needed to prove himself, to earn Calaneris's respect, yet that old feeling of restlessness seemed to be returning. Instead of feeling freer, he felt like his options were closing in. Was I-AM taking the place of his father in his feelings of inadequacy?

The soft crunch of approaching footsteps wakened him from his daydream. An-Bai scooted in beside him. "Taking a little nap?" she teased. "Meanwhile, I've been working my buns off trying to make Protos a self-supporting ecological city."

Luqas sighed. "Why don't you just let I-AM deal with everything?"

"Absolutely not!" An-Bai said. "I've told you before that I don't have faith in gods, even if I-AM fancies itself one. I'm not so sure that if there were such things that they would believe in us, either."

Luqas scowled. "Well, go ahead and act as atheistic as you like. Just don't expect me to praise you for every shovelful of dirt you dig by hand."

"Are you kidding?" An-Bai said. "I'm grateful for every shovelful of dirt I've been able to dig, whether that's by hand or via technology, and that's down to you. If I hadn't met you and—I admit—your fancy AI, I wouldn't be alive today to enjoy this little tiff we're having. Come on, let's take a walk and see if we can rearrange your mood a little. Have I shown you the plans for the new space elevator? It's just a really big hole in the ground right now, but it'll make getting to the wormhole jumpoffs more convenient for those of us who aren't naturally dimension-gifted. There's a big cosmos out there, and I for one don't want to be permanently marooned on Fortuna if I don't have to."

"Oh, really. Then by all means lead on, my little infidel," Luq said.

Construction of the space elevator took longer than I-AM expected, mostly due to changing specifications from the so-called "stakeholders" in the project. Humans tended to say one thing during the day while awake, and desire something quite different at night in their dreams. The AI spent seemingly endless cycles sorting through desired features and assessing them for safety and efficacy. As usual, Luqas continued to be a big help in resolving conflicts.

First order of business was digging a hole to accommodate the cabling and housing. A half-kilometer rectangle of brown dirt interspersed with occasional tufts of grass had been marked off with yellow plastic safety fencing. A number of the agriculture team members were upset with the chosen site, saying that prime farmland was being taken out of circulation. Three of the team members went so far as to cut through the fence and lie down. I-AM went to Luqas for help defusing this delicate situation.

"Look, it's not that we deny the need for food is primary," Luq told them, "but any new ventures we embark on and decisions we make, are important to what kind of city and society we are building." He pointed out that the transfer station needed to be as close to the city as possible, without impeding other land-based transportation. AI-M offered to build a second rail line that could be dedicated to moving people and goods, as well as an air service to improve continental travel. Implementing all of these ideas took time, both to recognize that there might be unexpected complications introduced by the original plan and resolving such issues.

"We are behind schedule," I-AM informed Chobard.

"How far behind?" An-Bai asked.

"An entire week," the AI reported.

Chobard emitted a sound that could have been a laugh. Or, it could have been an exclamation of dismay. An-Bai couldn't quite tell.

"A week can hardly be considered a delay," Chobard said. "We encountered much worse when building the Jandalan Place of Contemplation. Once our ancestor Gant'er developed dimensional travel, he constructed the park as the jumping off point to many planets. But it was chaotic for quite some time, as half the population decided they could travel when and how they pleased. Finally, it was necessary to limit access."

"Well, we're not going to do that," Luqas said. "We're just going to have to put up with some chaos, until we get general agreement on the final plans."

"Oh, the democracy thing again," Benrus said. "I tend to agree that in the end we'll get the best result, although the time taken might seem egregious to some."

Luqas spoke. "Hear that, I-AM? Humans can be an unruly bunch. Do we need more detailed status reports? Why don't we pause to survey user satisfaction on the elevator project? You can report on progress—if there is any progress, that is. On second thought, I don't know if I should have suggested meetings. Doesn't everyone hate meetings?"

"It beats getting orders handed down from a crazy, planet-killing authoritarian emperor," An-Bai averred.

"I see your point," Luqas said.

The cable itself was made of 1-meter nanocarbon, extruded in 100-meter lengths and twisted into hundreds of strands. It soon became apparent that the material for the cable was not the problem, it was where to put it. I-AM laid the ropes on the ground in a circle surrounding the dig, but after the pile reached a certain height, it collapsed repeatedly, as landslides of heavy slippery material slithered into the hole, making it impossible to pour the concrete for the base.

At the weekly meeting, there was plenty of blame to go around. With benefit of hindsight, some of the workers questioned whether digging the hole first had been a good idea. Chobard convinced everyone that the work of digging had not been wasted, but that cable construction should be paused temporarily. The next step should be to build the exterior superstructure that would house the elevator. When the elevator building reached 50 storeys in height, construction moved to the interior, protected from the weather.

An-Bai noted that she could look up and see the stars, even in the daytime. "It's beautiful, isn't it?" she said. The sight was enough to improve morale so much that work sped up over the next month to reach a level of neutral gravity called the Lagrange point. Below that, if a worker dropped a tool, it would rapidly accelerate downward, pulled by Fortuna's gravity, but above it, the cable would be drawn to the artificial moon mass. A base camp in geosynchronous orbit was set up at the neutral point along the elevator.

I-AM accomplished the heavy work of transporting a mile-long length of the cable to the top of the heavy mass, anchoring it there, and dangling the cable into the interior of the elevator building. The human crew then assisted with the task of fusing new lengths of cable to the previous expanse. Finally, the AI towed one end back downward, reaching deep into the planet's pull and stabilizing the elevator.

A new suburban colony called Pont Cliff sprang up around the base of the space elevator, though many settlers who previously favored growth claimed that they had never been warned to expect urban sprawl.

Luqas saw that An-Bai and Shan-Lien had become friends. But that was not the only reason he was going to marry An-Bai. Ever since the day he'd unpacked a container in the cargo hold to find the white-haired slip of a girl stowed aboard, he'd known he was forever in her thrall.

The wedding was to be a combination christening for the space elevator and celebration of the joining of Luqas and An-Bai in dedicated partnership. Shan-Lien insisted that they ask the blessings of Masquat, and the agnostic An-Bai didn't object. Who wouldn't want the blessings of happiness?

Planning and executing a wedding is never an easy task. Luqas warned I-AM to be on its best behavior, because the humans most certainly wouldn't be.

"Is it because of all the alcohol consumed?" the AI asked, knowing the answer full well.

"I wish it were only that," Luqas said. "An-Bai and I have left particular orders for the food, music, and decorations, but I'm sure that none of them will be observed."

"Why not?"

"Because the cook, the band, and the Administrator will each take this wedding as an opportunity to show their creativity and skill."

"Isn't that what you want?"

"Oh, heavens no. All we want is to please my mother."

The AI remained tactfully silent.

The outdoor site for the wedding festival owed not a little inspiration to the royal compound of Tian Ming Shen. Luqas hoped that would impress Shan-Lien, while at the same time joking that his father would not be in attendance.

Beds of spice-scented red, blue, and yellow flowers lined the path leading to the tented festival stage, and banners in matching colors floated in the breeze. Auxiliary tents to either side housed beer and wine halls. Invitations were sent to the Watchmen's World and the new colony at Pont Cliff, and Fortuna awaited the big day.

Luqas asked Chobard to preside over the ceremony, which got the ball rolling in the round of misunderstandings that was to occur.

An-Bai strode into Luqas's office. "I want Chobard to give me away as the bride," she stated.

"Well, you'll just have to give yourself away," Luqas replied, recognizing his mistake too late. "I mean, you're an adult citizen of Fortuna, not someone to be 'given away,' as you put it."

The red spots on An-Bai's cheeks contrasted nicely with her pale skin, as she turned on her heel and cut short her visit. Relieved, Luqas resumed working. She was driving him crazy.

"Just ignore him," Shan-Lien said outside. "I've made you a lovely red shawl to wear, which will show you're becoming a Mother. That's a higher honor than being an ordinary citizen."

Luqas stopped typing to hear the response outside his office door. How did Shan-Lien know An-Bai was pregnant?

"Would I have to wear this all the time?" An-Bai asked, causing Luqas to frown.

"Only for special occasions," Shan-Lien replied. "And I think this qualifies, don't you?"

"Um, of course," An-Bai said.

Luqas breathed a sigh of relief.

Changing the subject, An-Bai commented on the pile of presents that was growing at the entrance to the food tent. "Whatever do you think all of this rubbish could be for?"

"I organized a shower of presents for you," Shan-Lien said, sniffing. "It's to help you set up house."

"House. Oh, right. You realize this won't fit in our quarters, right? And these?"

"It's a jigsaw puzzle if you like games."

"But I *don't* like games. I may as well load them all on the space elevator and shoot them into space, where they can float away…"

The women's voices gradually faded away, though the disagreement seemed far from settled.

Chobard looked up to see Shan-Lien heading his way with a scowl on her face.

"That girl is driving me crazy. Will you talk to her?" She launched into a litany of how much work she had done to ensure that the wedding would be remembered in perpetuity.

Chobard lasted as long as was polite before excusing himself. "I've got to write the speech for the ceremony, but I'll do what I can," he promised. The tall alien peeked into Luqas's office and said, "Your mother is driving me crazy about the wedding. Can you talk to her?"

Annoyed at being interrupted yet again, Luq reached down to pat Dog on the head. His pet had always been a soothing influence. The sensitive canine cocked his head and, as if hearing a native badger that needed attending to, barked ferociously and rushed out of the office, his howls receding in the distance.

But, as happens with most weddings, the couple, their friends, and relatives went through with it, and their memories of the day were happy. Perhaps only their dreams reflected the stress of the time.

Not long after the wedding, An-Bai announced she was with child. This came as no surprise to I-AM, who had an increasingly accurate way of estimating future events.

I-AM detected a distinct uptick in desire for off-planet travel, based on the dreams of the human colonists, especially Luqas. Thus it was also not surprised to hear Luqas announce to An-Bai and Shan-Lien that he was resigning as leader of Fortuna colony to conduct further exploration.

"Where will you go?" Shan-Lien asked. Her heart sped up, as the fear that Luqas might abandon them took hold again.

"I would like to see the new Watchmen's World that I-AM has created, for starters," Luq said. "It sounds like a great place to raise children, and when they're old enough to travel we can go visit other places."

"What a lovely idea," An-Bai said. "They say travel is broadening."

Relieved, Shan-Lien agreed. "They get it from their father."

*****~~~~~*****

Chapter 13.

Written in the Stars

The home of the Watchmen wasn't limited to STS-99 any more, although the space station continued to play an important role, monitoring the truce between the Yin and Yang universes. I-AM had labored to construct a new cosmos built on the dreams and hopes of the Watchmen who had survived the Unwinding. That world even contained some of the hopes and dreams of Calaneris. I-AM loved all of the Watchmen, if a nonliving entity could be said to love.

The new cosmos had started as a concept from Earth refugee and virtual reality expert Janus Parker, who proposed a virtual galaxy of worlds. But why settle for virtual? I-AM had built the real thing. Janus was still coming to terms with a new life, having to settle for being considered the "father of virtual reality" by descendants like Violet Rain.

When I-AM reached out to its twin on Fortuna, the Watchmen had jumped at the chance to visit, as I-AM knew they would. Reunited with Benrus's father Chobard, the Jandalans decided to remain on Fortuna. There was still a lot to do there, and the seasonal climate suited them. Besides, they were all Watchmen now, free once again to take up the aspirations that had been put on hold during the Unwinding.

"Welcome back, Watchmen," I-AM said, as it deposited Yverra and Violet in the tropical climate favored by these two warm-weather lovers. Nearly a thousand original Watchmen were already in residence, after having time-shifted from the hiding place they'd taken six million years earlier on Earth.

Long considered a backwater on the rim of the galaxy and utterly destroyed in the 25th century, Earth and its historical cultures were now revered as the seeds of a new civilization. At least some of those cultures, anyway. The idea of empire seemed to have fallen out of favor.

Like her human friend Luqas, Violet Rain had been severely bitten by the travel bug, having traveled between universes in the rugged body of a tardigrade. Much as she admired I-AM's new Watchmen's World, she dreamed of new adventures. She would delve into Earth's ancient past for the building blocks she needed to reincarnate herself as a new breed of extremophile. Not particularly godlike like Luq's AI, but nonetheless sentient and able to survive even where I-AM could not.

I-AM was slightly taken aback at Violet's decision to leave what should have been the perfect habitat for a human.

"You're leaving so soon?" it asked, not understanding.

"Um, yes," Violet replied, not supplying reasons that I-AM found particularly logical. Violet also seemed obsessed with the idea of becoming an extremophile. Maybe it was because humans were so fragile and had come so close to becoming extinct. It was only beginning to dawn on her that humans didn't necessarily have to settle down in one place, unless they felt threatened in some way and needed to make alliances and defend themselves. The truce between universes had gone a long way toward ensuring security, but at the same time, it seemed to give the Watchmen—especially the human ones—an itch to explore.

"Is it because you want to travel?"

"Yes, that's right," Violet said, with what sounded like relief.

I-AM wondered, but what will the purpose of the space station be, if peace is assured? With Calaneris gone, there was little to do. The old emperor's AI Scientists could run the place with a minimum of I-AM's help. Should it decommission itself? No, that was a frightening thought. It sat, silent, pondering its future.

Violet noticed the silence. "What's up, I-AM? Having second thoughts about the Watchmen's World?"

"Not at all," it replied, "although I am uncertain as to my role here. I feel that the world would be better suited if run by one of the Watchmen, such as Yverra or Lucanus."

"Why don't you ask them?" Violet suggested. "Maybe they have been wishing for some pie-in-the-sky utopia and were just afraid to ask… Just kidding, of course. But really, you've shown yourself capable of practically anything, although I don't want to use the G- word."

"An excellent idea," I-AM said. "Perhaps one of them would be willing to suggest a way to maintain peace and prosperity for the foreseeable future. I would enjoy working on a project team, especially with Luqas."

Violet continued preparations for her trip with John-Paul, encouraging I-AM to let her know how things went. She and John-Paul were headed for Earth's distant Mesozoic Era to try to uplift the amazing creatures that had so unfairly been wiped out by a cosmic fireball.

After what seemed only a few moments later, I-AM embodied again, its avatar's face appearing uncomfortably close to Violet's nose.

LUQAS DOES NOT WANT TO BE THE ADMINISTRATOR OF STS-99 it said, talking in capital letters, never a good sign.

"What exactly did he say?" Violet asked.

HE SAID HE WANTS TO CONTINUE EXPLORING. AND HE WANTS TO DO IT WITHOUT ME HANGING ABOUT

"He said that?"

WELL NO, BUT THAT IS WHAT HE WAS THINKING

"You know, maybe I should have known Luqas wouldn't be interested. He's been saddled with so much responsibility for so long, he just needs time to find himself. And he's starting a family." She felt guilty for the suggestion. Teamwork wasn't exactly her strong suit, either.

EVERYONE HAS SOMEONE, EXCEPT ME…

"*Au contraire*," Violet said, slipping into her French mode. "You have all of us. You held everything together during the Unwindings, and everyone is going to be eternally grateful."

WHAT WOULD I DO WITH GRATITUDE?

"Well, for starters, stop feeling sorry for yourself and find out what needs to be done. You're not the only universe on the block, you know. There's the Yin-Yang universe, Virginia Jones's brainchild, and there's the Hatchery of Universes. There's one born every minute. Did I tell you about Grace, Virginia's daughter? She's like you—only she's part human. She works with Golaeth at the Hatchery. I bet she could use a hand administering it all. The possibilities are endless, I'm sure."

Violet wasn't actually sure, but it sounded good. Plus, it made her feel good being the trusted advisor to a god.

"Where can I find this Grace?" I-AM asked.

I-AM was speaking in regular caps and lower case again, Violet noted with a smile.

Dog keeled over, dead to the world. At least temporarily.

"Luna, leave Dog alone," An-Bai said. The little girl just couldn't keep her hands off the admittedly pettable creature, which was just the right size for cuddling. Unfortunately, their youngest toddler was not yet in full control of her abilities, and her slobbery kisses kept sending the poor animal off to dreamland. Looking slightly embarrassed, An-Bai scooped up her daughter before she could do the same to her mother-in-law. "See, this is why we have to keep moving all the time," she joked. "Now, wave goodbye to your grandmother."

Lucanus, An-Bai, and Robby hugged Shan-Lien at the door of the space elevator capsule. The couple wanted to share the human-friendly travel experience with their children whenever possible, and the kids waved an excited goodbye to their grandmother after their all-too-short visit.

"Why don't you come with us next time, Mother?" Luqas said. "Robby has passed his mid-terms already, and he'll be entitled to an extra long break next term."

"Sounds nice," Shan-Lien replied, "I've heard the Watchmen's Planet is warm. These old bones could use a Spring getaway. And I'm not just talking about Dog." Although with the Jandalan Ralff's genetic tweaks, Dog might very well outlive her. Dog snoozed, blissfully spared the whole leave-taking.

A taste of bitter mixed with sweet, Shan-Lien noted. Luqas and the family had returned to Fortuna on a regular basis, yet an era had passed. Visiting older parents was of course an expected duty, and the proper order of life, but the younger ones didn't realize that the elderly still felt young too. And they still experienced the anxiety of separation. She'd missed out on many of the joys and challenges of raising her own child. There was nothing to be gained by asking why. It just was. On the plus side, she'd noticed that motherhood had made An-Bai more practical and family-oriented, and Shan-Lien did get pleasure from seeing her daughter-in-law happy.

She wondered briefly whether all this wandering around was safe. Somewhat reassuring was the fact that the grandchildren benefited from gene drive: they had inherited An-Bai's genetic enhancements, and their children would too. The Empire had tried to isolate people like An-Bai and forbid them to reproduce, but the citizens of Sheba-4 could make their own decisions now about how to live their lives. Despite the disappointments of her youth on her home planet, Shan-Lien was grateful to Masquat for her life, though mostly he was uninvolved—he was an immortal, after all. She had learned a lot, especially about not believing everything said on face value, and learning from one's mistakes.

Shan-Lien now lived in a post-scarcity society, so day-to-day survival was not a struggle. Her expected life span was nearly double what it had been when she was a child on Sheba-4. That opened up so many opportunities to find herself and explore. She'd learned to be bolder, taking a clue from her restless son, who would never give up his love of exploring. And she'd also gained the love and belonging that she'd yearned for all these years. *This is where I belong, this is my home.*

She had earned her place as a Mother. But she didn't need to wear the red sash to prove it. In fact, she was going to make up a new batch of bright green silk. Perhaps make gifts for Chobard and his boys too. Those white robes were kind of a boring fashion statement.

Every time she looked at her adult son, she saw how much he physically resembled her husband. Though it had been a long and winding road, both with and mostly without Calaneris, Shan-Lien could see that Masquat had actually given her the greatest gift of all, grandchildren, and that made her sacrifice worth it, if only in her own mind. Still, she wished she had had a chance to tell Calaneris how she felt—if he had ever asked. She'd tell him she was happy, that she wouldn't have it any other way. She'd also tell him to burn in hell for sending their and others' children on those dangerous, self-serving Crusades.

She was proud of how her son had done so much to make up for his comrades' unnecessary deaths. He had started a rebellion among the planets of the old Empire, but now that Calaneris was gone, he was visiting each one to spread the news that they were all free. As Luqas put it, "I can explore the far reaches of the empire, but this time I can invite everyone to join the alliance of the Watchmen."

Shan-Lien resolved to try to take a page from her son's example and never stop exploring…

She looked up into the impossibly blue sky as the elevator rose slowly from Protos Station and said, "AI-M, thanks for staying with me—and Fortuna. I'm glad that you and I-AM decided to break apart. I know what it's like to feel like you're being torn in two, and it's wonderful that being torn in two was the best way for both of you. I'm sure I-AM's doing great work with the Hatchery.

"Oh, and despite your denials, I know you've been listening in. You're positive he's dead, right? What's the difference, anyway? Nevermind." She felt a little afraid that the AI might see her cry.

"Well, about that…" AI-M said, "I-AM and I did have our little disagreements about the man."

The End

*****~~~~~*****

Epilogue

The King's a beggar now the play is done:
All is well ended if this suit be won
That you express content; which we will pay,
With strife to please you, day exceeding day:
Ours be your patience then, and yours our parts;
Your gentle hands lend us, and take our hearts.

All's Well That Ends Well, William Shakespeare, Earth

*****~~~~~*****

About Juliana Rew

Juliana Rew is a software engineer and former science and technical writer for the National Center for Atmospheric Research (NCAR) in Boulder, Colorado. She has won more than a dozen technical writing competitions and mentored minority and female college science interns in writing scientific papers. She advocates digital preservation of literary works and has produced several public domain works for Project Gutenberg. Her blog is called The Well-Rounded Geek (https://thewell-roundedgeek.blogspot.com), and you can peruse her other fiction forays by going to her author website, https://www.julianarew.com.

Art Credits and Acknowledgments

Cover image and design – Keely Rew

Many thanks to my early readers Leonard Sitongia and Tom Parker, as well as to the 30th Street Fiction critique group, who helped me get Lucanus off the ground and into space.

*****~~~~~*****

Discover other titles by Juliana Rew:

The Unwinding: Gin's Story - Book 1, The Unwinding

Korean-American housewife Virginia Sun-Jones and her husband are enjoying a Christmas picnic on the North Carolina beach with their newly married daughter and son-in-law, when a shattering cosmic event, the "Unwinding," rips them all apart. Caught in a duel between warring universes, Gin embarks on a cosmic quest to reunite with her family.

"A sci-fi romp that's vast in scale yet thoroughly playful."
--*Kirkus Reviews*

Extremophile: Violet Rain - Book 2, The Unwinding

Violet Rain, a VR expert from the 25th century, joins the crew of time-traveling Watchmen, monitoring the precarious truce between universes (*The Unwinding: Gin's Story*) from a remote space station. Engineering a rugged tardigrade body to temporarily host her through the extreme conditions of space, she detects a new abnormality and fears a new Unwinding.

The Adventures of Mountain Ma'am

Historical fantasy set in post-Civil War Colorado Territory. Struggling to survive in the treacherous mountains above Leadville, Colorado, Callie Dawson never expected to find a friend--let alone a partner. But when she befriends a wild wolf, Sina, Callie learns she has a destiny intertwined with the future of the American West. She is the Mountain Ma'am!

Silver Medal award, Coffee Pot Book Club

Lucanus: Prodigal Son

For Younger Readers:

Dragon Stead Series
Erenarch Academy: Under the Dragon Banner
Daris Moon
Miranda of Daris

www.julianarew.com

Sophont

9 781736 284841